Acting Edition

I0591807

The Keen Collection

One-Acts
by Contemporary Playwrights
Volume 9

A Little Bit of Tea with That...
by Bleu Beckford-Burrell

Bake Sale
by Stephanie Swirsky

Hatch
by C. Quintana

ǀǀSAMUEL FRENCHǀǀ

A Little Bit of Tea with That... Copyright © 2022
by Bleu Beckford-Burrell
Bake Sale Copyright © 2022 by Stephanie Swirsky
Hatch Copyright © 2022 by C. Quintana
All Rights Reserved

THE KEEN COLLECTION: VOLUME 9 is fully protected under the copyright laws of the United States of America, the British Commonwealth, including Canada, and all member countries of the Berne Convention for the Protection of Literary and Artistic Works, the Universal Copyright Convention, and/or the World Trade Organization conforming to the Agreement on Trade Related Aspects of Intellectual Property Rights. All rights, including professional and amateur stage productions, recitation, lecturing, public reading, motion picture, radio broadcasting, television, online/digital production, and the rights of translation into foreign languages are strictly reserved.

ISBN 978-0-573-71014-8

www.concordtheatricals.com
www.concordtheatricals.co.uk

FOR PRODUCTION INQUIRIES

UNITED STATES AND CANADA
info@concordtheatricals.com
1-866-979-0447

UNITED KINGDOM AND EUROPE
licensing@concordtheatricals.co.uk
020-7054-7298

Each title is subject to availability from Concord Theatricals Corp., depending upon country of performance. Please be aware that *THE KEEN COLLECTION: VOLUME 9* may not be licensed by Concord Theatricals Corp. in your territory. Professional and amateur producers should contact the nearest Concord Theatricals Corp. office or licensing partner to verify availability.

CAUTION: Professional and amateur producers are hereby warned that *THE KEEN COLLECTION: VOLUME 9* is subject to a licensing fee. The purchase, renting, lending or use of this book does not constitute a license to perform this title(s), which license must be obtained from Concord Theatricals Corp. prior to any performance. Performance of this title(s) without a license is a violation of federal law and may subject the producer and/or presenter of such performances to civil penalties. Both amateurs and professionals considering a production are strongly advised to apply to the appropriate agent before starting rehearsals, advertising, or booking a theatre. A licensing fee must be paid whether the title(s) is presented for charity or gain and whether or not admission is charged. Professional/Stock licensing fees are quoted upon application to Concord Theatricals Corp.

This work is published by Samuel French, an imprint of Concord Theatricals Corp.

No one shall make any changes in this title(s) for the purpose of production. No part of this book may be reproduced, stored in a retrieval system, scanned, uploaded, or transmitted in any form, by any means, now known or yet to be invented, including mechanical, electronic, digital, photocopying, recording, videotaping, or otherwise, without the prior written permission of the publisher. No one shall share this title(s), or any part of this title(s), through any social media or file hosting websites.

For all inquiries regarding motion picture, television, online/digital and other media rights, please contact Concord Theatricals Corp.

MUSIC AND THIRD-PARTY MATERIALS USE NOTE

Licensees are solely responsible for obtaining formal written permission from copyright owners to use copyrighted music and/or other copyrighted third-party materials (e.g. artworks, logos) in the performance of this play and are strongly cautioned to do so. If no such permission is obtained by the licensee, then the licensee must use only original music and materials that the licensee owns and controls. Licensees are solely responsible and liable for clearances of all third-party copyrighted materials, including without limitation music, and shall indemnify the copyright owners of the play(s) and their licensing agent, Concord Theatricals Corp., against any costs, expenses, losses and liabilities arising from the use of such copyrighted third-party materials by licensees. For music, please contact the appropriate music licensing authority in your territory for the rights to any incidental music.

IMPORTANT BILLING AND CREDIT REQUIREMENTS

If you have obtained performance rights to this title, please refer to your licensing agreement for important billing and credit requirements.

TABLE OF CONTENTS

ABOUT KEEN TEENS

Founded in 2000, Keen Company is an award-winning Off-Broadway theatre producing stories about the decisive moments that change us. Central to Keen Company's mission is to present theatre that patrons can identify with and connect to. The Keen Teens program is the cornerstone of the company's outreach and educational efforts, bringing the company's values to the high school stage by developing new work tailored specifically to teen actors and audiences.

When first creating Keen Teens in 2007, the company found that teachers did not have access to material intended for a high school stage. Educators were left to present either classic plays never designed for teen actors, or material created specifically for school groups that lacked richness or relevance. Through Keen Teens, the company began commissioning original plays and musicals that are as complex and multilayered as the lives of high school students today, penned by accomplished professional playwrights and musical theatre writers.

There are two components to Keen Teens: The first is a free program for New York City-area high school students to work alongside professional writers, directors, and designers to rehearse and premiere these plays Off-Broadway. The second is that the plays then go on to be published and licensed through our partners at Concord Theatricals as *The Keen Collection*.

The Keen Collection is made up of comedies, dramas, and musicals; scripts range from the sincere to the absurd, from the existential to the most intimate. Some deal head-on with topical issues, others simply aim to provide smart, contemporary material. These original pieces have been created by many of the most talented writers working today, including Bekah Brunstetter, Kristoffer Diaz, Madeleine George, C.A. Johnson, Greg Kotis, Mike Lew, James Tyler, Leah Nanako Winkler, and Lauren Yee. This group includes finalists for the Pulitzer, Wendy Wasserstein, and Susan Smith Blackburn Prizes; and winners of the Yale Drama Series Prize, Horton Foote Playwriting Award, and more. Their theatrical work has been produced professionally on and off Broadway, and their writing has reached an international audience on TV shows including *Girls*, *GLOW*, *Mad Men*, *Mozart in the Jungle*, *Nurse Jackie*, *Tales of the City*, and *This Is Us*.

As well as being tailored to the social and emotional world of teens, these plays are also designed to be accessible in educational settings. All scripts run thirty minutes, with simple design elements, large ensembles, and flexible casting requirements. Each play can be presented on its own or in combination with other *Keen Collection* titles on a shared bill.

Keen Teens has made possible the Off-Broadway debut of over three hundred young actors and has led to the publication of over thirty-five new one-act plays and musicals, which are regularly produced not only

Keen Teens has made possible the Off-Broadway debut of over three hundred young actors and has led to the publication of over thirty-five new one-act plays and musicals, which are regularly produced not only in the United States, but in countries around the world, from Australia to Singapore.

For more information, please visit www.keencompany.org/teens.

Keen Teens Staff

Molly Meador, *Artistic Producer*
Lindsay Warnick, *Associate Producer / Production Stage Manager*
Jeremy Stoller, *Director of New Work*
Celestine Rae, *Director of Education*
Ashley Scott, *Associate Director of Education*
Jeremy Stoller, *Director of New Work*

Keen Company

Jonathan Silverstein, *Artistic Director*
Ashley DiGiorgi, *Managing Producer*

Design Team (For all Projects)

Devon James, *Set Designer*
Jennifer Chi, *Costume Designer*
Victoria Bain, *Light Designer*
Julian Evans - *Sound Designer*

KEEN TEENS AMBASSADORS

Keen Teens is generously supported by the Axe-Houghton Foundation, as well as a group of donors affectionately called the Keen Teens Ambassadors:

The Axe-Houghton Foundation, The Marta Heflin Foundation, Irida Amati, Marsha Dietlin Bennett, Stephanie Bok, William and Cynthia Bradford, Maria Brause, Kyle Cardone, Elizabeth Corradino, Timothy Conlon, Rose Courtney, Alexander Cox, Bill Craco, Linda D'Onofrio, Amyt Eckstein, Amy Glass, Barbara Gottlieb, Tim Grandia, Mike Griot, Maureen Hart, Bao Ho, Sally and William Huxley, Haley Huxley, Frank Iryami, Charlie MacLeod, Emily MacLeod, Jeremiah Maestas, Oren Mandel, Marsha Mason, Maria Pulsoni-Cicio, David Rabinowitz, Kayam Rajaram, Kilburg Reedy, Kitab Rollins, Alan J. Rose, Michael Rose and Heidi Hoover, Courtney Renee Sargent, Nisha Sheth, Olga Staffen, Marjolein Steenbergen, Randy Strickland, Louise and Ernie Stringer, R. Lee Stump, Dan Swern, Stephanie Swirsky, Jason Tam, Emily Wexler, Shauna Weinberg, Louly and Bill Williams, Pia Winslow, Kara Winslow, Emmy Zuckerman and Ed Bonfield

A LITTLE BIT OF TEA WITH THAT...

by Bleu Beckford-Burrell

A LITTLE BIT OF TEA WITH THAT... premiered on May 20th, 2022 and was produced by the Keen Company. The performance was directed by Mark Cirnigliaro. The cast was as follows:

ALLISON	Nina Luyindula
ZOEY	Lesly Montano
KRISSY	Samatha May
OLI	Karla Lazala
CARMEL	Oscar Giles
GARREN	Chinua Baraka Payne
SELINA	Quinn Canales
MARTIN	Zakariah Massoud (Zak)
ROSE	Michelle Lambe
MR(S) SANTIAGO	Tovi Lisker

CHARACTERS

ALLISON – Black, 15/F, conscious loyal and dedicated friend and student.

ZOEY – P.O.C, 15/F, very confident, social butterfly and has just found a little bit of popularity

KRISSY – White, 14/F, takes boy crazy to another level and definitely has a phone addiction.

OLI – Black, 15/F, tom-boy, foster kid, just looking to have a good time.

CARMEL – White, 16/M, debate team captain with a strong sense of moral obligation.

GARREN – Black, 17/M, a nerd with a passion for Track & Field.

SELINA – Latinx, 18/F, overworked, night manager struggling to keep work, school and family life in order.

MARTIN – Latinx, 16/M, pariah. Works as the busboy for the café.

ROSE – White, 16/F, great work ethic with questionable loyalties.

MR(S) SANTIAGO – Latinx, 40s/M or F, overworked high school teacher.

AUTHOR'S NOTES

Selina can be played by any (P.O.C) child of an immigrant all other racial identities unless noted are not interchangeable.

(A small Mom-and-Pop café still surviving in the changing Williamsburg neighborhood on the border of what is considered the "good side" of town and the "bad side" of town. Across the wall is painted "A LITTLE BIT OF TEA WITH THAT", the café feels like the inside of a warm country kitchen. The area exists for seating with tables and chairs, a register to the side with small snacks, and stools line the adjacent wall. A walkway leads to the back area, for the café kitchen and staff lounge.)

*(**MARTIN** wipes down the tables and sweeps the floor as **ROSE** daydream by the register, she eventually notices **MARTIN**, and stares at him for an uncomfortable amount of time.)*

ROSE. You think it's true?

MARTIN. Huh?

ROSE. Do you think it's true?

MARTIN. You talking to me?

ROSE. *(Looks around the empty café dramatically.)*

MARTIN. Right. Right.

ROSE. So, do you?

MARTIN. Do I what?

ROSE. Do you think it's true?

MARTIN. I don't know what the "it" is.

ROSE. You know, at school today...the whole...you know... and you know...you know what I'm talking about.

MARTIN. No, I don't really know. No one exactly tells me anything.

ROSE. But you have to know!

> (**MARTIN** *shrugs, goes back to sweeping.*)

> (**ROSE** *Looks around to make sure no one is around, as she walks cautiously to* **MARTIN.** *She whispers in his ear.*)

MARTIN. *(Drops the broom, mortified.)*

ROSE. Wow, you really didn't know? I guess, I shouldn't ask if you know who said it?

> (**ALLISON** *with an insanely large backpack, holding a number of books, enters backway in the café, somewhat muttering to herself.* **ROSE** *dashes to the register as* **MARTIN** *picks up the broom, still a bit out of it.*)

> (**ALLISON** *turns around, looks at all the tables she can't decide where to sit. She walks over to each table trying to measure the distance from, the door to the table. She finally gives up and drops her books on the table, while assuring herself she's picked well. She removes her backpack and jacket. Sits down, checks the time on her watch, and stares at the entrance.*)

ROSE. Hi Allison.

ALLISON. *(Still peering at the entrance.)* Hi Rose.

ROSE. Welcome to A Little Bit of Tea With That, do you need a menu or would you like your usual? We have a brand-new tea, if you'd like to try it.

ALLISON. What kind?

ROSE. Vanilla-Honey Chamomile, known for it's soothing and calming effects.

ALLISON. Does it have caffeine?

ROSE. Mm, hold on. I'll be right back. (ROSE *heads to the back.*)

> (MARTIN *gathers himself and returns to sweeping, suddenly notices* ALLISON *sitting down. He intentionally sweeps around her like the moon orbiting the earth. Every so often sneaking long wishful gazes.*)

> (ALLISON *looks at her watch, stands up, sits down, stands up again, sits down.*)

ROSE. Ok, there isn't any caffeine in the new tea, but it smells delicious.

ALLISON. No thank you. I think I'll have my usual.

ROSE. Alright, coffee, black, steaming hot, no nothing added, just extra hot fresh black coffee.

ALLISON. Thanks.

ROSE. Martin.

MARTIN. Huh?

ROSE. Here. (*Hands* MARTIN *the order and return to the cash register.*)

> (MARTIN *takes the order to the back.*)

> (KRISSY *bursts into the café, beelines to* ALLISON.)

ALLISON. Finally!

KRISSY. Oh my god Ally, you're not going to believe this!

ALLISON. Wait, where's Zoey?

KRISSY. How should I know?

ALLISON. It's already 5:33 you both were supposed to be here at 5:30. I got here at 5:28, you two really need to work on being punctual. What if this was a job interview? What if it was life or death? What if –

KRISSY. Yeah, yeah, yea, no one is dying Ally, relax. Anyways, have you been on IG?

ALLISON. You know I only use my phone from 7:30pm to 9pm, to keep my studies and social life balanced. Focus is key, did you know there is a study that shows eighty percent –

KRISSY. *(Shoves her phone into* ALLISON *face.)* Mikey liked my picture! This is the 3rd time in one month, I'm not crazy, he has to like me. He's so cool and cute. Did you see his haircut this week? Look. *(She pulls up a picture of Mikey.)*

MARTIN. *(Brings coffee over to the table, whispers.)* Allison, here's your coffee. *(She doesn't hear him, he whispers again.)* Hey, Allison your coffee is ready. *(She doesn't hear him, he stands awkwardly holding the coffee.)*

KRISSY. Look at this one, *(She's endlessly swiping.)* And this, oh my gosh. How can God make a creature like this? Oo, and this. *(She suddenly looks up and notices* MARTIN.*)* Ally is that for you?

ALLISON. *(Turns around.)* Oh, yea my coffee. Thanks, Martin.

MARTIN. *(Whispers.)* You're welcome, Allison.

ALLISON. Huh? Did you say something?

MARTIN. THANKS, WELCOME ALLISON! *(He dashes to the back.)*

　　　　(Beat.)

KRISSY. That dude, is so weird...but is it me or his voice sounds deeper? I like it. Mmmm. I wonder if he has a girlfriend. You think he has a girlfriend.

ALLISON. You don't even know his name.

KRISSY. Um, A-little-bit-of-tea-with-that-guy.

ALLISON. Martin.

KRISSY. Whatever. You think he's on TikTok? Guess who just did a duet with me?

ALLISON. *(Opens up a book and starts writing.)* No.

KRISSY. C'mon it's no fun without you guessing.

ALLISON. No thanks.

KRISSY. Just three. Just three guesses. Please, please, pretty please with coffee on the side.

ALLISON. Fine.

KRISSY. Ok, first guess.

ALLISON. *(Without looking up.)* Mickey-John-Peter.

KRISSY. Hey! Ally that's not –

ROSE. Hi Krissy.

KRISSY. Hi.

ROSE. Welcome to A Little Bit of Tea With That, do you need a menu or would you like your usual? We have a brand-new tea, if you'd like to try it.

KRISSY. Is the tea pretty, like TikTok or IG worthy? Will it be plated?

ROSE. Um, no, sorry. It does smell delicious though.

KRISSY. You guys should really, get with the times. I feel like it's been the same since like the 90s or something. You know the café on South 9th plates their tea they make cute petals out of colored whipped creams with little chocolate chip flakes on the rim of the saucer. I posted it, and I got like 102 likes from it.

ROSE. Wow, that's a lot.

ALLISON. Is it?

KRISSY. No, of course not but Phillip, left a comment that said "Yum". Just give me the, yoosh.

ROSE. Got it. French vanilla, Ice coffee, 2 shots of espresso with 5 scoops of sugar, with a little iddy bitty drop of soy milk.

> (**KRISSY** *gives her the thumbs up.*)

ROSE. *(Looks around for **MARTIN**.)* Martin!

> (**MARTIN** *quickly comes from the back grab the order and quickly returns to the back.*)

ALLISON. Have you started your global history project? I'm really thinking about Ancient Greece and modern-day society, similarities...

KRISSY. Ew, this is why we don't hang out that much anymore. Seriously, homework? It's spring break, and there is soooooo much going on right now I can't even – Ahhhh! Zoey!!!

ZOEY. *(Slowly enters the café, she is dressed in the best and latest fashion trend.)* Heyyyyy. Krissy, I saw that Mikey duet, good for you. Ally –

ALLISON. You are so late, Zoey. I don't think you respect time at all.

ZOEY. Time, waits for me and anyone else who demands it. I read that somewhere.

ALLISON. Where? I can add it to my reading list.

ZOEY. Life. By Zoey.

KRISSY. *(Laughs.)* That was a good one.

ALLISON. Ha ha, very funny.

ROSE. Hi Zoey.

> (**ZOEY** *turns to **ROSE** and smiles.*)

ROSE. Welcome to A Little Bit of Tea with that, I can give you a menu if you'd like, we have a new tea today if you'd like to try, it smells delicious.

ZOEY. Hmm. Can you tell me what's on the menu?

ROSE. Sure, I can bring a menu if you like.

ZOEY. No, I'd rather you just tell me, actually, what teas do you have?

ROSE. Well, we have Oolong, Green, Herbal, White, Black, Yellow, and Fermented.

ZOEY. Yea, but what kinds?

ROSE. The most popular amongst our peers is herbal. We have twenty-five different kinds.

ZOEY. Wow, twenty-five that's a lot, I'm sure you know all of them, right?

ROSE. Of course.

ZOEY. Ok... I'm listening.

ROSE. *(Takes a deep breath.)* Anise, bearberry, chamomile, honey chamomile, cinnamon, elderberry, eucalyptus, garlic, ginger, ginsing, honey, hops, jasmine, kava, lemon, lemon grass, mugwort peppermint, orange peel, passion flower, raspberry, rosemary, sassafras, strawberry, and violet. They're all really good.

ZOEY. Oh. Just give me a glass of water, no ice.

ROSE. No problem. *(Gets cup of water.)*

ALLISON. Zoey, really?

ZOEY. What?

KRISSY. That was a little bit –

ZOEY. Ridiculous.

ALLISON. Yes.

ZOEY. Yea, they need to work on customer service in here.

MARTIN. *(Brings over Ice coffee.)* One Ice Coffee.

KRISSY. Thank you. Wait, you're a senior right?

MARTIN. No, I'm, I'm, I'mma junior.

ZOEY. Do you make a lot of money?

ALLISON. Zoey!

KRISSY. I heard waiters can make a lot of money.

ALLISON. It's none of our business.

ZOEY. Well, do you?

MARTIN. I'd rather not answer that question.

ZOEY. I was just trying to give some advice, I've noticed you staring at Ally.

KRISSY. What? When?

*(**ZOEY** puts her hand up to shush **KRISSY**.)*

ALLISON. Martin, don't pay attention to her, she's –

ZOEY. All, I'm saying is if he wants your attention, he should probably use his money to fix himself up. Get a haircut, buy some news clothes, trust me it's not about the brand but the swag. Maybe walk a bit straighter, if not, stop staring, would you?

MARTIN. I wasn't, I didn't, I mean, I'm sorry if I made you uncomfortable. *(Gives an apologetic look to **ALLISON**.)*

ZOEY. You did. Now go, before I tell your manager. And where's my water?!

ROSE. *(Appears with the water, smiling.)* Would you like anything else?

ZOEY. Thank you, is your manager here?

ROSE. She hasn't got in yet. No.

ZOEY. Please tell her, I'd like to speak to her when she comes in.

KRISSY. Can I get another straw?

ROSE. Sure and of course. *(Quickly gets the straw and returns to the register.)*

ALLISON. What is wrong with you?

ZOEY. What? I'm looking out for you. He's always being creepy in school, during 4th period but you're so oblivious to everything, you don't even notice. You should be saying thank you. I saved you from a sociopath.

ALLISON. *(Whispers.)* Maybe you're a sociopath.

ZOEY. What was that?

ALLISON. I am not oblivious! That's why I asked to meet here today. I notice things.

KRISSY. Welllllll, you didn't notice my duet with Mikey and he liked three of my posts! Aren't we best friends?

ALLISON. This is an intervention.

ZOEY. Wow, someone is being over-dramatic.

ALLISON. No, I'm not. Zoey, you're a mean girl.

ZOEY. Ok.

ALLISON. Krissy, you're extremely self-centered.

KRISSY. What? No, I'm not. I just want everyone to like me.

ZOEY. We aren't in middle school anymore, we can't spend all our time reading books and day-dreaming about characters, and places we've never been to. We're in high school now and our image, is more important than, not hurting some loser feelings.

KRISSY. Well, maybe he's not a complete loser, he does have a job. But Ally, we're your friends and people say things about you.

ALLISON. You mean people spread rumors? Huh?

KRISSY. Exactly.

ALLISON. Like the one today?

KRISSY. Yes!

ZOEY. You don't want that to be you, do you?

ALLISON. No, Zoey I don't.

ZOEY. So, maybe you should start listening to us, instead of intervening and judging our life choices.

ALLISON. Did you make up the rumor?

ZOEY. Excuse me?

ALLISON. Did you make up the rumor about, Selina?

ZOEY. Wow.

KRISSY. *(In a whisper.)* Ally, take that back. Zoey, she doesn't really think that you could do such a thing.

ALLISON. Maybe you were a part of it too, Krissy.

KRISSY. What?!

ZOEY. *(Pointedly.)* Selina, probably could have saved herself, if she would lighten up a bit and stop parading around the school as if she's the next coming.

KRISSY. Plus, is it even a rumor? It's true isn't it? She's always wearing long sleeves and turtle necks. Who wears turtle necks anyways?

ALLISON. You think she deserves everyone thinking she's being physically abused by her parents?!

ZOEY. You should lower your voice.

> *(CARMEL enters causally, wearing slacks, button-up and tie. CARMEL takes a seat at one of the empty tables.)*

KRISSY. Hey, Carmel!

> *(CARMEL gives the piece sign.)*

ROSE.   ZOEY.

(Takes **CARMEL**'s *order*   Krissy, this is not the time
and hands it off to   to be social.
MARTIN.*)*

KRISSY. Um, Carmel is super charismatic, he destroyed
Prep Academy last week at the debate, you think
he'll do a quick Live with me? *(***KRISSY** *walks over to*
CARMEL.*)*

ALLISON. But she isn't self-centered?

ZOEY. Self-centered or not, you have no right accusing us
of talking about Selina or making up things about her.

ALLISON. You still haven't said you didn't start it.

ZOEY. I shouldn't have to, Selina is a nobody to me. I
wouldn't even waste my time. You know what? I have
nothing to say to you until you apologize.

ALLISON. You threw your water at her last month because
there was a speck on your ice.

ZOEY. It spilled, and I said I have nothing to say to you.

ALLISON. Fine! *(Grabs all her belongings and sits at one
of the stools.)*

KRISSY. *(Returns to the table with* **ZOEY**, *showing the video,
she just did.)* Does my forehead look big?

ZOEY. Not now, Krissy.

KRISSY. Seesh. *(She uses her phone to consider her
forehead.)*

SELINA. *(Enters in a storm of fury.)* The nerve, the nerve,
the nerveeeeeee. *(She goes straight into the back.
Offstage.)* Rose! Martin!

> *(***MARTIN** *hurries to the back.* **ROSE** *heads to
> the back but is quickly cut off by* **ZOEY**.*)*

ZOEY. Don't forget to let her know I'd like to speak to her.

ROSE. Right, I didn't forget.

ZOEY. Great. *(Takes a seat and reapplies mascara.)*

(Back hallway in front of the Staff Lounge.)

ROSE. Is everything alright, Selina? You're pretty late today.

SELINA. No, everything is not alright.

MARTIN. Can we do anything to help?

SELINA. Sure, you can tell me who started the rumor today?

ROSE. Rumor?

SELINA. Don't act stupid Rose, this is not the time.

MARTIN. I think she's talking about the one you told me earlier.

ROSE. Hush, Martin.

SELINA. So, you know something Rose?

ROSE. No, I don't know anything. Well, I know what was said.

SELINA. I'm guessing you don't know anything Martin but Rose, I know you just work for me and we aren't like friends or anything but if you know who started that rumor about me... I'd really appreciate you telling me.

ROSE. Nope, can't say that I know anything. But if you gave me like a paid day off. I could try and find out.

MARTIN. Rose, that's not cool.

ROSE. Oh? So, you don't want a day off while being paid, to not see all our classmates and enemies' smug faces?

MARTIN. Well, yea but not like that.

SELINA. Just shut up, both of you. Do you have any idea what it's like to have your parents investigated and question about beating you up! They would never do that, they would never treat me or anyone like that. This is the worse thing that could ever happen.

ROSE. I'm sorry for being insensitive but I have to get back on the floor. Also, Zoey at table two wants to speak with you to make a complaint.

SELINA. What?

ROSE. Zoey –

SELINA. I heard you, the same girl that threw water at me?

MARTIN. The same.

SELINA. I honestly hate her and I hate this day!

ROSE. OK, well I'm gonna go now. I hope...your day gets better. (**ROSE** *goes back to the front.*)

SELINA. *(Emotional upset.)* Sometimes I think Rose is a robot, with no feelings at all.

MARTIN. I'm sorry. When she told me, about it earlier I had no idea...the school contacted your parents?

SELINA. Nobody understands what I'm going through. This is my worst nightmare.

MARTIN. I mean, can't you just say, it's not true and then everything goes back to normal?

SELINA. My mom, my mom, she's she's not...

MARTIN. Not what?

SELINA. She's not a legal resident. Now what if they take her away because someone thought it was funny to say, my parents are abusive. My parents never do anything, in fear they may cause unwanted attention. Never, and now this.

MARTIN. Do you think you should be at work right now?

SELINA. No Martin, no I don't, but I have to I help my parents pay for things. I don't have the luxury all of you have to work or not work just because.

MARTIN. I'm sorry.

SELINA. Just get back to work.

MARTIN. I'm really sorry Selina.

SELINA. Just go.

> (**MARTIN** *heads back to the front and takes out the garbage.*)

SELINA. *(Takes a few moments to compose herself, and goes straight to* **ZOEY***.)* Hi, I was told you would like to speak to the manager.

ZOEY. Yes, one of your employees *(Pointing at* **MARTIN***.)* was making my friends and I very uncomfortable, he was staring rudely.

SELINA. I apologize, for your discomfort I will have a word with him and please have a cup of tea on behalf of A Little Bit of Tea with That.

ZOEY. I don't want a tea.

SELINA. No worries, your order will be on us.

ZOEY. What if I don't order anything?

SELINA. Your next order.

ZOEY. What if you're not here?

SELINA. I'll give up a coupon. You can use it whenever, now or later.

ZOEY. Fine.

SELINA. Glad, I could help. *(She goes to the back taking,* **MARTIN** *with her.)*

KRISSY. Aw, man. I'm a little hungry can we use that freebie now?

ZOEY. No. Did you file the complaint, or did I?

KRISSY. Whatever, it's fine I'm doing a food-free diet so my cheeks look contoured without makeup. *(Takes selfies of her sucking in her cheeks.)*

ZOEY. Good luck with that. *(Now applying lipstick and gloss.)*

> *(**GARREN** enters wearing athletic wear, there is something a little off about his walk but in a idiosyncratic way. He looks around and waves to the entire café, makes a stop at the register.)*

GARREN. Hey...

ROSE. Hi, welcome to A Little Bit of Tea With That.

GARREN. Hi, ah, um, can I, can I um, can I get a hot chocolate? *(Pays for hot chocolate.)*

ROSE. Not a problem. *(Brings order to the back.)*

GARREN. *(Approaches the table with **CARMEL**.)* Hey...

CARMEL. *(Sipping tea, gives the piece sign.)*

GARREN. Were you here long?

CARMEL. Time is only noticed by those who waste it.

GARREN. Wow, that was deep. I'm glad we're doing this history project together, I need to get an A.

CARMEL. I'm sure you could achieve that without me.

GARREN. *(Chuckles.)* Yeah right. I checked out your debate tournament last week. I wish I could sound like that when I speak, charismatic. Like a president or something. Why do we need to orally present our project anyway?

CARMEL. Speech, the spoken language, is currently under attack my friend.

GARREN. *(Laughs.)* I'll never sound like you even if it weren't under attack.

CARMEL. It's nothing, just practice. Rumor has it that you have the fastest time for the 100 meter.

GARREN. No way, second fastest but that's not my favorite race. You ever think about joining the track team.

CARMEL. No time.

GARREN. A lot of practice sounding like the president huh?

CARMEL. Exactly, "practice makes perfect" classic adage, a maxim for the soul.

GARREN. *(Takes out his notebook and a stack of index cards.)* I bet if I sounded like you did, people would listen to me more...coach, the teachers, shoot even my parents they'd all finally listen.

CARMEL. No success comes out of fear. *(Takes out laptop.)*

GARREN. *(Notes the laptop.)* I'm not afraid, I just know my strengths and weaknesses.

CARMEL. Everyone fears something, what are you afraid of?

GARREN. ...seriously?

CARMEL. Yeh.

GARREN. ...girls...definitely girls...and doing this history project with Oli today.

CARMEL. Aha! Girls are easy once you conquer the oral language. Oli on the other hand a little more complicated.

CARMEL. Stand up.

GARREN. What?

CARMEL. Stand up and pretend you just entered and I'm a girl *(Looks around the café)*. Pretend I'm...pretend I'm Zoey.

GARREN. Hell no. *(Immediately sits back down.)*

CARMEL. Too challenging?

GARREN. Just an unlikely scenario.

CARMEL. Only thing unlikely is what we don't believe in. Alright, *(Looks around again.)* Allison.

GARREN. *(Gulps.)* Alli-al-ally *(Stammers.)*

CARMEL. Ooook, maybe too close to home. C'mon pretend I'm any girl.

GARREN. *(Turns his chair to face* **CARMEL***.)* Ok.

CARMEL. Ok. *(Girly voice.)* Hi, Garren you look super cute in your track uniform!

GARREN. I'm not wearing my uniform.

CARMEL. But you *are.*

GARREN. Oh, right. Ah, thanks. I hope it doesn't smell, I sweat a lot after a race.

CARMEL. *(Girly voice.)* Oooo, you must be really fast then?

GARREN. Uh, um, ah yeah? Uh ah, um, A.J. he's a senior has a way better time than me.

CARMEL. *(Girly voice.)* A.J.?

GARREN. I can introduce you to him.

CARMEL. Ok-ok-ok-ok, let's stop. You want to introduce a girl to *you!*

GARREN. I'm hopeless.

CARMEL. No. We need real stimuli *(Points to* **ROSE***, as she approaches them.)* her! Get her, to give you, her handle.

GARREN. What?! Are you crazy?!

CARMEL. Yes, as are all geniuses. Do it!

ROSE. *(To* **GARREN.***)* Here's your hot chocolate. Would you like anything else?

CARMEL. *(Nudges* **GARREN.***)* Actually, he does.

GARREN. Uhumah hi! My name is Garren.

ROSE. I know, we have English together, first period.

GARREN. Uh, ah, right, um, right. Social media is fun right? I use it!

ROSE. Ok.

GARREN. But-bu-bu-but, I was thinking um that ah um, you use it, right?

ROSE. I'm sorry I don't understand what's happening. Would you like anything else?

> *(***CARMEL*** shakes his head "no" profusely for* ***GARREN*** *to see.)*

GARREN. Yes, um, ah *(Sputters causing his hot chocolate to spill on his notebook.)* I need your handle please.

ROSE. Oh my gosh, *(Hands napkins to* **GARREN***, genuine.)* I'm so sorry, my cousin suffers from a stutter, he's in speech therapy. It's really been helpful, so don't worry it gets better. So much better, you won't have to rely on social media anymore. I appreciate you sharing that very personal story. *(Pats* **GARREN** *on the shoulder.)*

GARREN. Ah...thanks.

ROSE. *(To* **CARMEL.***)* Would you like anything else?

GARREN. I was ju-ju-just –

CARMEL. No, no, thank you, we won't need anything else.

> *(***ROSE*** returns to the register.)*

GARREN. *(Whimpers.)* I can't believe that just happened.

CARMEL. How about I treat you to another hot chocolate. Didn't mean to embarrass you.

GARREN. Absolutely not, she can _not_ come back over here.

CARMEL. I need to make it up to you somehow.

GARREN. *(Picks up soggy notebook.)* Print me out the history notes.

> *(CARMEL helps GARREN dry the pages of his notebook. As SELINA comes from the back. And brings coupon over to ZOEY.)*

ZOEY. Thanks, I thought you forgot.

> *(SELINA ignores ZOEY, heads to the register and empty the bills into the money bag. She gives a thorough check of the Café, (all is in order) she returns to the back.)*

ZOEY. *(To KRISSY.)* She's really not going to apologize?

KRISSY. Who?

ZOEY. Allison!

KRISSY. Oh, that's what we were waiting for?

ZOEY. Why else would I be in this crap-box for so long?

KRISSY. Because it used to be our favorite hangout spot.

ZOEY. Not, anymore. Come on. Let's go.

KRISSY. We're leaving Allison?

ZOEY. You can stay if you want.

KRISSY. Well, I just feel like...

ZOEY. Mikey's, supposed to be there.

KRISSY. Really? Wait, where?

OLI. *(Struts into the café, wearing a backwards cap, chewing a gum more like a straw way too intensely.)* Well, well, well, little miss thing, Krissy the missy, that's your handle right? *(Completely invading KRISSY's personal space, by looking at her phone.)*

KRISSY. You already know that.

OLI.
Just teasing girl, relax. *(Beat boxes while doing a trendy dance.)* We should hang out some time.

(MARTIN brings out mop bucket and caution sign, heads over to GARREN and CARMEL. MARTIN freezes when he notices OLI. ALLISON turns around to face OLI.)

ZOEY. *(Grabs KRISSY by the arm.)* No thanks, anyways we were just leaving.

OLI. But I just got here! The spot...the hang out spot! Martin! *(Sings the MARTIN theme song and laughs at her own brilliance. She grabs MARTIN in a choke hold, ruffles his hair then slaps him on the back.)* Martin, my man! Still being the biggest creep, in Williamsburg?

ALLISON. Leave him alone.

OLI. Relax, nerd. Martin and I go way back. Isn't that right Martin?

ZOEY. *(To ALLISON.)* You'll defend him but not us?!

OLI.
ooOoo, trouble in paradise.

(MARTIN tugs himself away from OLI's grasp.)

ALLISON. Zoey, you're not a victim.

OLI. OoOh! She said you ain't a victim!

ZOEY.
Shut up Oli!

ALLISON.
Shut up Oli!

OLI. Oh, so everyone wants to look at me like I'm a bad guy, man go back to drinking your hot beverage. Ay, *(To ROSE.)* give me whatever... *(Points at CARMEL.)* that one is having. *(She struts over to CARMEL and GARREN table.)*

ZOEY. That's it we're leaving, Allison you've obviously chosen a side.

KRISSY. *(Hurt for the first time.)* How could you accuse us, when people like *(Towards* **OLI.***)* that exist?

ZOEY. Let's go. I'm over her and I'm over this. *(Exits the café with* **KRISSY** *on her heels.)*

OLI. Ay! Where you going? Nobody needs them anyway. Am I right or am I right? Stuffy, boogie females. You need to play some music in this joint, borinnngggg! *(Sits on the table.)* Boys, boys, boys, boys, boys, how's my A coming along on this hissssstory project? Ready for *oral* presentations?

CARMEL. Real mature.

GARREN. We-we-we don't want any problems Oli.

OLI. Problems? Problems? Too bad my middle name is trouble. *(Snatches some of the index cards off the table.)* or did you forget Garrrreennnnnn?

CARMEL. I think perhaps, you have forgotten. I know your entire name and none of them is trouble.

OLI. *(Spiking one card at a time at* **GARREN.***)* ooOoooooOOooo, Carmel the savior, Carmel Mr. effing Superman over here. Is Daddy Warbucks gonna come and save me too?

GARREN. *(Picks up the index cards.)* um, ah, um, we-we need those for the project.

CARMEL. Flanagan's don't get saved.

GARREN. *(Pauses picking up index cards.)* Actually, Oli I-i-i think you meant Lex Luther, not Warbucks, both are rich but Lex Luther is in the DC universe and well Warbucks is a fictional character from the musical *Annie.*

OLI. *(Laughs hysterically, then mocks.)* Lex-luther-blah-di-blah-da-DC-universe *(Plops down into the chair.)* what a waste of fine specimen you are, beauty and too much brain. *(Toss the rest of index cards on the table.)* I'm def getting an A.

SELINA. *(Enters from the commotion.)* Excuse me, you'll have to bring it down or leave the café. You're disturbing the other patrons.

OLI. My bad, you got it. *(Gestures zipping the lips.)* hey, you that girl, right?

SELINA. Excuse me?

OLI. *(Circles* **SELINA** *looking her up and down.)* Oh shoot! You are that girl. *(Raps.)* Moms and Pops putting hands on you – aka physical abuse – black and blue – you look like you bruise easy too – C.P.S. say no no boo – damn I got bars! But for real for real, man, I'm sorry about your family situation, don't worry foster care has its perks. Makes you tough, bold and a fighter. Some people say, bully. I say strong. Keep your head up. Next time your mom or dad come after you just *(Mimes an upper cut and jab.)* give them that.

SELINA. GET. OUT.

OLI. What?

SELINA. Leave now.

OLI. What I say? I'm trying to do a good deed, do you a favor, give some solid advice. Besides, I'm not going anywhere, where's my drink?

CARMEL. Oli, you should just go.

OLI. I'm not going anywhere. I'm a paying costumer. *(Rubs fingers together for money, to* **CARMEL**.*)* You got me, right? Besides, I always earn my keep *(Props one foot up on the table.)* gotta do my part for the project.

SELINA. *(Barely keeping her composure.)* MARTIN!

OLI. Yeah, "Martin!"

MARTIN. *(Brings out hot chocolate.)* Here you go, one hot chocolate. (**CARMEL** *pays* **SELINA**.)

> (**OLI** *takes the hot chocolate makes a show of taking a sip.* **SELINA** *hisses and storms off to the back.*)

> (*Carrying a large box,* **MR(S) SANTIAGO** *struggles getting into the café, takes a look around, and notices* **OLI** *and tries to escape.*)

OLI. *(Spots* **MR(S) SANTIAGO***, runs over and blocks the door.)* Heyyyyy, Mr(s). Santiago, you look like you can use some help? Let me help.

MR(S) SANTIAGO. No, no no! It's ok, Oli I'm alright. I don't need any help. I'm fine, really, I'm fine.

OLI. Don't you want a hot beverage of something? You didn't even order anything and you leaving?

MR(S) SANTIAGO. I changed my mind.

OLI. Hey, I'll treat you, if you change my grade on that last paper. How about you change my grade I get you a drink? What you want tea, coffee, hot chocolate? They got marshmallows. *(To* **ROSE***.)* You got marshmallows, right?

> (**ROSE** *nods.*)

MR(S) SANTIAGO. No Oli, no I will not change your grade. I've said no on multiple occasions, when you plagiarize you will receive a zero. I will not change your grade on a paper you did not write yourself. The answer is No! If you spent as much time as you do, trying to bribe for a grade you don't deserve on your paper you wouldn't be in this situation. Enjoy your break and please don't speak to me again about this. *(Exits.)*

OLI. Wow! Discrimination. *(To no one in particular.)* Right? How she know I didn't write the paper, Huh? Cause I use some S.A.T. vocabulary? Cause Oli can't be smart? Oli can't be like you?! *(In* **ALLISON** *face,* **GARREN** *jumps up.)* or what, like, mister Wikipedia over here with all the fancy ties and perfect eloquence! I know things. I know lots of things and one day I'mma have the last laugh.

SELINA. *(Holding an open kettle, storms over to the register.)* Oli get the hell out of my cafe!

OLI. Don't talk to me like that! You don't run things! You don't own this.

GARREN. *(Steps in front of* **ALLISON** *in a protective stance.)* Hey, hey calm down. Relax.

CARMEL. Look obviously, you're going through something why don't we go for a walk?

GARREN. Yea, yea. Or a run, running always takes things off my mind, you know? Burn some energy...some anger...

CARMEL. Come on, Oli. No one thinks you're dumb, just you know, a provocateur.

OLI. Yea, provocateur or not I deserve respect.

SELINA. Oh, comfort the trouble-maker, when I'm the one going through things. Do you see me acting like a fool, making a scene?

CARMEL. Someone has to act like an adult.

SELINA. I'm tired of acting like an adult, I've been acting like an adult my entire life! *(Yells.)* Who started the rumor?! Who spread those lies about me?! I know one of you know, I know!!!

ROSE. Oh my gosh, Selina calm down.

OLI. *(Laughs.)* No one's gonna tell you, and you don't deserve to know, cuz to them, you're just a dirty little beaner!

GARREN. *(To OLI.)* Whoa, Let's get out of here.

OLI. Yeah, I said it!

SELINA.	*(OLI jumps out of*
Oh yea?! *(Throws the tea at OLI.)* How bout a little bit of tea with that?! Chamomile to calm your ass down!	*the way just in time, as* **GARREN** *and* **MARTIN** *heroically dive in front of* **ALLISON**.*)

ROSE. Selina, stop. *(Drags SELINA to the back.)*

OLI. That's why the person who started that rumor is right in your face and you don't even know it!

    (CARMEL begins to pull OLI out the café.)

GARREN. *(To ALLISON.)* Are you ok?

    (ALLISON nods.)

GARREN. Phew! I'm glad you didn't get hurt.

ALLISON. Me too. Garren, right?

GARREN. Yea?

ALLISON. What's your handle?

GARREN. WB.LightenBolt.

ALLISON. Cool, I'll add you.

CARMEL. *(Struggling to pull OLI out, to GARREN.)* Little help here.

GARREN. Sure! *(To ALLISON.)* Later! *(Helps CARMEL pull OLI out the café, they exit.)*

    (Beat.)

ALLISON. Oh my god, that was crazy.

MARTIN. Yea, it was.

ALLISON. You think she was telling the truth?

MARTIN. ...what do you mean?

ALLISON. You think Oli was telling the truth, that the person is, was just in here that started the rumor.

MARTIN. I don't know, it's Oli.

ALLISON. Yea, but I don't think she's a liar. A bigot yes, liar I dunno, I think she sees things differently and think she's funny but... I don't know...what if she's telling the truth?

MARTIN. So, what if she is? I mean, what I mean is why does it matter to you?

ALLISON. Cause I might owe someone an apology. I think I may have made really terrible accusations and I should make things right.

MARTIN. What if you didn't mean to, or what if you thought you were right, or maybe you didn't realize what you were doing?

ALLISON. What do you mean?

MARTIN. ... Nothing, never mind.

ALLISON. Martin, what are you saying? Do you know anything about the rumor being started? If you do you should say something, lots of people are being hurt from it.

MARTIN. I...I...can't... I mean...I didn't...I don't...I'm sorry.

ALLISON. Why are you sorry? You can tell me, I won't get mad.

MARTIN. I'm sorry. It was during 4th period Bio lab, when you know, Zoey said, I was being a creep. You were working with Selina and I was kind of staring. I didn't mean to stare, I was just done with writing my data and I guess, I looked in your direction a little too long because Zoey came up to me and asked to copy my answers. But I guess I didn't hear her at first. And she asked was I staring at you and I said, No. I was looking at Selina's turtle neck. And then Oli overheard and made a joke saying, "Only people that wear turtle necks and shades when it's out of season, have one kind of problem" and I didn't want Zoey to keep saying I was staring at you so, I said yeah, people trying to hide something, like marks or something. And Zoey asked doesn't Selina wear them all the time and I said yeah like every day, you'd probably think her parents hit her or something. But I didn't mean it, like I didn't think it was a fact and I don't know who else was listening, it could have been anyone sitting near me. But I just felt embarrassed caught looking at you, I just wanted to change the topic. I didn't lie or anything. I didn't think it was a big deal.

ALLISON. Martin, you have to tell her.

MARTIN. How? She'll be so angry, she might fire me.

ALLISON. You have to apologize and you need to make it right. You played a part in this whole thing and it's gotten way out of control.

MARTIN. I know, but what if she doesn't believe me. I wasn't trying to be malicious.

ALLISON. No, you were trying to protect yourself and got someone else hurt.

MARTIN. But I didn't spread it. I didn't go around telling people Selina parents are abusive.

ALLISON. No, you didn't but you lit the match that started the fire. You could have just said, you were looking at me, it would have been fine. I've always thought you were a nice person I wouldn't have cared. And now, I have to put out the fire I started with my friends because of this. You need to do the right thing, Martin. *(Picks up her belongings and begins to exit.)*

MARTIN. Wait!

> (**ALLISON** *stops in her tracks.*)

MARTIN. Don't apologize to them.

ALLISON. *(Turns around.)* Excuse me?

MARTIN. Would they apologize to you? Would they apologize to anyone? Zoey walks all over everyone who stands in her way and Krissy is just a blind follower. They don't even see you or listen to you, am I wrong? I…see you…

ALLISON. They're my friends and I'm choosing to believe them, Martin. If you really saw me, you would've spoken up in class, and owned it. Not used Selina as a cover… I really liked you Martin and now… *(Shrugs.)*

MARTIN. Last month, every day you brought a bag lunch to school and every day you waited in the lunch line for a second lunch and gave it to Alexis Crawford, while everyone else just makes fun of the holes in her clothes. Last summer, I saw you in the community garden with those old people, filling their baskets with tomatoes and fruits and your smile, even ol' Sam who swings his cane at everyone. And my first day in this city, I remember it was raining and I dropped my signed copy of *My Hero Academia*, it was ruined. I felt someone tap me on the shoulder and it was you, Allison, you saw me standing over this soggy, dirty, filthy, deteriorating mess and you said, "Hey, is that a?" and I interrupted you and said –

ALLISON. "No! No, it's not a comic book ok!"

MARTIN. Right, and you said, "I was going to say manga is that an anime manga?"

ALLISON. And you said, "Yea, *My Hero Academia*"

MARTIN. I'll never forget what you said after that –

ALLISON. "I heard manga's are special like a fairytale for adults and kids alike because no matter what happens, to us, the characters, there's always something to be happy for when it all comes to an end. This is just a part of the journey, it'll get better."

MARTIN. That's who you are Allison, that's who I see everyday a selfless, generous, beautiful person, who'd stop whatever she was doing, just to make a strange boy day better.

ALLISON. ... I don't, I don't know what to say...what do you want me to say?

MARTIN. Tell me I'm not crazy, say...you've felt the same way too, say you understand.

ALLISON. –

MARTIN. ALLISON?

ALLISON. Yes...ok. You're not crazy, I like you, I really liked you more than just a friend and I don't know I thought maybe...maybe one day you'd do something, and now... everything is just messed up!

MARTIN. It doesn't have to be –

ALLISON. But it is and I think you just don't understand, you could have approached me a long time ago! And now you've ruined everything.

MARTIN. This is what happened when I dared looking at you. Approach you? You knew, I liked you, it's not all my fault.

ALLISON. Stop trying to blame everyone else Martin, take some responsibility. That's what I'm doing and so should you.

MARTIN. Nothing I say or do will make this better.

ALLISON. I guess you're no better than what you think of my friends, huh? *(Shakes her head.)* I'm really disappointed in you...you need to tell Selina. *(Exits.)*

MARTIN. *(Whispers.)* I'm sorry. *(Puts his head in his hand...he is like this for a while. Sits up, stares off for a second.)* Selina! We need to talk.

    (Blackout.)

End of Play

BAKE SALE

by Stephanie Swirsky

BAKE SALE premiered on May 20th, 2022 and was produced by the Keen Company. The performance was directed by Sarah Krohn. The cast was as follows:

SUZIE	Charlotte Coffey
JULIA	Polly Gillmore
AUSTIN	Dereck Diller
IZZY	Beatrice Rimel
GRACE	Raizel Moscardon
ZOE	Milena Manocchia
LUKE	Oscar Giles
REBEKAH	Chelsea Paradiso
ARIEL	Sofia Fraidenraich
PRINCIPAL	Aidan Inwood

CHARACTERS

SUZIE – 16, she/her, considers herself a leader

JULIA – 16, she/her, committed to doing the right thing and also getting good grades

AUSTIN – 16, he/him, a practical thinker

IZZY – 16, she/her, powered up and ready to go

GRACE – 16, she/her, has anxiety and is primarily worried that everyone hates her

ZOE – 16, she/her, hates herself and understands if others do too

LUKE – 16, he/him, loves Jesus and his parents and most of all, himself

REBEKAH – 16, she/her, blunt and that's just how she is

ARIEL – 16, she/her, has a lot of energy and deeply cares about everything and everyone

PRINCIPAL – of uncertain age, any gender, runs the school

SETTING

A high school.

The blank void of digital communication.

Rebekah and Ariel's bedroom.

Scene One

(A classroom. Normally used for something like U.S. History. There's a map of the United States. Portraits of old dead white presidents. Maybe one that is alive too.)

(A group of a teenagers have organized themselves in a circle. They are all seated at the moment. They are talking through something that matters to them.)

(SUZIE, 16, calm and in control, addresses them all.)

(JULIA is talking to her friends SUZIE, AUSTIN, GRACE, IZZY, and ZOE, all 16, all juniors in high school, and all friends.)

SUZIE. That's how it started. I asked Bekeh in class. I said, to her, "Why are you selling Palestinian food? Can you just please clarify to me – have you spoken to any Arab students in the school to see how they felt about this?"

IZZY. And!?

JULIA. Then she said there aren't any Arab students in the school.

IZZY. Wow.

AUSTIN. Yo are there?

SUZIE. I saw her sign up because you know everyone but Julia and me are slacking on their bake duties.

AUSTIN. You said I could just show up the day of and help set up.

JULIA. "They can't govern themselves."

They. She can't even say Palestinians.

That made me feel like – oh. It's not just hummus and yeah pita.

AUSTIN. Yo what class was this. How did this come up.

JULIA. WAIT and then she added. "They're all terrorists."

IZZY. No...

(**IZZY** *is shaking her head.*)

SUZIE. YES. I was there!

AUSTIN. Damn. Did you say anything?

SUZIE. I was speechless. But Julia said, "are you serious" and was about to blow up –

JULIA. But then Mrs. Hudinski said we had to start class.

IZZY. I would have punched her in the face.

GRACE. And we used to all be friends with her. She changed.

ZOE. I think she was always...

(**ZOE** *doesn't know how to finish her sentence.*)

JULIA. What?

ZOE. I don't know.

(*A moment.*)

JULIA. Where's Luke?

AUSTIN. You think he's hooking up with her right now?

GRACE. I...I heard. Luke. Are his parents like big Republicans?

JULIA. – That's not fair to say because they have a lot of money.

GRACE. I don't mean to rush us but we didn't reserve this classroom for our emergency bake sale committee meeting and I'm worried a teacher will find us and give us all detention.

(**IZZY** *jumps up.*)

IZZY. So. The screwed up thing is that I don't think the school is going hold her accountable. I am not talking about detention or suspension. That is a slap on the wrist. And I am trying, honestly, to think about what that accountability looks like here. Certainly it's not she goes to a mosque and talks to members there. That's no. No. I am thinking out loud here.

AUSTIN. Yo it's a weird thing to sell at a bake sale. Hummus? You bake that?

IZZY. No. That is another great point.

GRACE. Well, the pita. You bake that.

IZZY. You don't claim something that isn't your own. That's the point, Grace.

(**IZZY** *is up now, pacing.*)

And then what she said! Not okay. Words have consequences. And her words are a danger to the Arab students in our community.

AUSTIN. But what if there aren't any? It's like the tree that falls in the forest. If it falls hard and no one is there, does it hurt anyone? No. Even if it falls really hard.

JULIA. *(To* **AUSTIN.***)* You're an idiot.

SUZIE. I'm selling apple pie, because America.

IZZY. Apple pie isn't actually American, you know that?

SUZIE. Really?

IZZY. English. But actually taken from the Danish.

> (SUZIE *doesn't know what to do with this information.*)

SUZIE. Oh! Well actually I am part, my dad's great grandfather is from like, Denmark.

GRACE. Are we – like we want her to sell something else?

JULIA. Luke and Bekah aren't hooking up. They're just hanging out. Barely.

ZOE. So. Actually. Can I share something?

> (*Everyone looks at* ZOE.)

I was going to go to Israel. Two years ago. With my family.

I'm Jewish. Like Bekah.

IZZY. We know, Zoe. We're not anti-Semites. Oh my God.

ZOE. No of course not. I wasn't.

SUZIE. We know you weren't.

ZOE. But no Bekah is Jewish too but I don't agree with her.

IZZY. Yeah no, and I get worried that like I can't – call out Bekah for calling all Arabs terrorists without saying I don't hate Jewish people. It's not a binary.

ZOE. So can I share something?

IZZY. Please do, Zoe.

> (IZZY *sits down.*)

ZOE. My grandmother – my dad's mom, she got sick. Like really – I mean she died. But it was right before the trip so my dad, he said we had to cancel. So we didn't go. And we didn't go another time. Like we just didn't go.

IZZY. Right. That's good – not about your grandmother. I mean.

ZOE. She was 85. So it wasn't like –

IZZY. – Still sorry. I didn't mean. I am sorry, Zoe.

ZOE. What I'm saying is that. Before – I was looking forward, like I was excited to go.

Cause I didn't realize.

Like, Jews always saying how Israel is our Homeland.

I believed that.

But actually Jews. Are wanderers. My family is from Poland.

GRACE. Maybe we can tell her to sell bagels.

ZOE. Actually interesting thing. I learned recently that bagels are Polish. It's a Polish food. It's weird because I did think it's a Jewish food. But Jews started having them in Poland. So it became associated with Jews, somehow, I guess.

But they – yeah because last year, my family, we decided to go to Krakow. Where my dad's family – my grandmother's mom, my great grandmother was born there. That's where bagels originated.

GRACE. Random...

I think she could still make them.

ZOE. The thing is – Judaism is a religion. But my family's ethnicity. We're white Europeans. So yeah maybe she could still make bagels but she still has to acknowledge that um like Israel isn't a valid country. Then yea maybe she could sell bagels.

JULIA. After class, like when we were packing up, she goes, basically out of nowhere, to Suzy and me, "my cousin was killed by a Palestinian terrorist."

AUSTIN. Yo what class was this.

JULIA. Calc.

ZOE. I have family there too. Some cousins. And I want to see them. But I don't feel right going there anymore.

> *(They all look at* **ZOE.***)*

AUSTIN. Sorry where?

ZOE. Israel. Well, really, Palestine.

> *(***LUKE,** *16, bounces into the room.)*

LUKE. – Hola mi compadres. Lo siento por mi tarde.

> *(***LUKE** *is clearly not a native Spanish speaker.)*

JULIA. You missed a lot.

> *(***JULIA** *likes* **LUKE** *but she's trying not to show it.)*

LUKE. Perra I know what she said.

JULIA. Are you hooking up with her?

> *(***JULIA** *quickly fails.)*

I just want to know if maybe you could have a sensible conversation with her.

ZOE. We should talk to the Principal. I can speak to how my family – and how they...are knowingly living on Palestinian land. They stole a Palestinian's family's home. They have been there awhile so it's not that my uncle literally stole the home but his uncle did. Some of my family are in the army and were even in the war in the 1940s. Just because millions of Jews, and other people, you know that other people were also slaughtered in the Holocaust. But all of this doesn't mean that you can go to another land and do the same thing in the name of saving yourself. I have thought about this a lot.

Now what you have to do is say that – Even though people have done wrong to me, I am not going to do wrong to others. I'll do nothing if it means not hurting someone. So no I am not going to sell Palestinian food. I am not going to sell anything. I'll buy. I'll support. That's all I do.

> *(Everyone in the room is moved.* **LUKE** *less so.)*

IZZY. That's accountability.

> *(They all snap their fingers in agreement.)*

Scene Two

(It's late at night. **BEKAH** *and* **LUKE** *text each other from their rooms in their homes, but also the blank void of digital communication.)*

REBEKAH. Hey

*(***LUKE*** looks at his phone. Thinks.)*

LUKE. Hola

REBEKAH. What are you up to

*(***LUKE*** thinks.)*

LUKE. Nada

REBEKAH. Yea

(A few moments.)

Can we hang out soon

*(***LUKE*** doesn't respond.)*

Ha

*(***LUKE*** thinks.)*

*(***BEKAH*** feels awkward.)*

(Then – **BEKAH***'s sister,* **ARIEL***, 14, walks into her room. They do share it, after all. Lights shift. We are out of the dark texting vortex.)*

*(***BEKAH*** looks at her sister, annoyed.)*

What!

ARIEL. This is my room too.

REBEKAH. Yeah but it's nicer when you're not here. Cleaner too.

You're a dirty ho.

(**BEKAH**'s *looking at her phone.* **LUKE** *hasn't responded.*)

ARIEL. Everyone hates you.

(**BEKAH** *doesn't say anything.*)

Do you know.

(**BEKAH** *looks at* **ARIEL**, *says nothing.*)

That.

(**ARIEL** *gets closer to* **BEKAH**.)

They think you're a problem addict for selling hummus and pita at the bake sale.

REBEKAH. What are you talking about?

ARIEL. PROBLEMATIC. But problem addict because you're addicted to causing problems.

It's so funny.

Oh also calling Palestinian terrorists. Which they are but. You don't say that, Bekah.

REBEKAH. I meant Hamas. And they are.

ARIEL. Everyone hates you.

(**BEKAH** *hits* **ARIEL**.)

REBEKAH. Just go away.

ARIEL. Resorting to violence. Wow.

Exactly what everyone expects of you.

I'm hungry.

I'm going to eat...food. Chicken.

Imma made chicken actually *schnitzel* for us for dinner and it's in the fridge and I'm warming it up and I'm eating all of it.

REBEKAH. Warmed up schnitzel sounds disgusting.

ARIEL. I love Germans and their food. Even if they once hated us. And killed us. Well not us because we aren't German. But it doesn't matter because now their food is MINE. YUM.

(**ARIEL** *smiles widely. Then leaves the room.*)

Scene Four

(As the scene transitions, an announcement comes from the loud speaker. It's the **PRINCIPAL.***)*

PRINCIPAL'S VOICE. *(Offstage.)* Students, please be aware that we do not allow emotional support animals at school. This includes hamsters.

(School hallway. The next day.)

*(***GRACE** *goes running down the hall, her phone in hand, looking down – and literally runs into Ariel, who was also looking down at her phone.)*

GRACE. Aah so sorry!

ARIEL.	**GRACE.**
Grace hi.	I'm so late sorry – I –

*(***JULIA***'s voice can be heard off-stage.)*

ARIEL. I wanted to ask you a question about the drama club meeting this week.

JULIA. *(Off-stage.)* I was so nervous. So nervous.

*(***SUZIE** *is rubbing* **JULIA***'s back as they walk on – followed closely by* **IZZY, ZOE** *and* **AUSTIN.***)*

(They see **GRACE** *and* **ARIEL.***)*

GRACE. Sorry. I meant to. I don't have an excuse. For being late. With the Principal.

JULIA. Ariel.

ARIEL. Hey. I was just talking to Grace about drama club.

(No one says anything.)

ARIEL. Julia, actually, are you coming to our meeting on Thursday?

JULIA. No.

ARIEL. Yeah I don't know if I can go either.

> *(An awkward moment. Then,* **ARIEL** *hurries off. She's gone.)*

AUSTIN. Shoulda told her that she can't sell hummus either.

ZOE. I would have said something but I didn't know what she was trying to do.

AUSTIN. She's not really like her sister. She's more fun.

IZZY. Ugh Austin you so obviously are drooling.

AUSTIN. Ariel's nice.

ZOE. I don't really trust her. Just right now, with everything.

> *(On the school's loudspeaker's a voice beckons. It's the* **PRINCIPAL** *again.)*

PRINCIPAL'S VOICE. *(Offstage.)* Rebekah Mofaz. Rebekah Mofaz to the Principal's office.

> *(The Group takes this in. It's real now.)*

IZZY. This is good. We are holding her accountable.

> *(The Group takes this in. It's real now.)*

JULIA. Where's Luke? He said he'd be here.

GRACE. He's lame.

JULIA. You were late too.

IZZY. He's a Republican.

JULIA. He can't vote...

IZZY. His parents.

> (**JULIA** *is embarrassed.*)

AUSTIN. Yo if that's [all] – I need to skip. K?

IZZY. Are you scared to see her?

> (**AUSTIN***'s already gone.*)

JULIA. LAME!

> (*Suddenly,* **REBEKAH** *is there. She isn't happy to be there. She's anxious.*)

REBEKAH. What do you want from me?

> (*She's trying to be bold but she's shaking inside.*)

JULIA. We all heard you, Bekah.

REBEKAH. I said Hamas.

SUZY. No you didn't specify.

IZZY. Why didn't you all record this? You need to record this.

> (**IZZY** *takes out her phone.*)

REBEKAH. Please don't record me. You don't have my consent to record.

> (**IZZY** *puts down her phone.*)

I really just wanted to sell hummus and pita. It's my dad's recipe.

ZOE. This is not about hummus. You used to do this all the time in Hebrew School.

REBEKAH. I think you just hate me so you're making stuff up.

PRINCIPAL'S VOICE. *(Offstage.)* Rebekah Mofaz. Rebekah Mofaz to the Principal's office.

REBEKAH. I have to go.

> *(A moment.)*

But um yeah it is really hard to feel bad for people who are doing bad, or just like attacking you. Like Hamas. Hamas are terrorists. They killed my cousin.

ZOE. It's not right to call people who are fighting for their basic freedoms "terrorists." Were the people in the Warsaw Uprising terrorists? They fought back. And now we worship them because they were fighting for their basic freedoms and were stripped of their citizenship and homes and families –

REBEKAH. – You can't compare the conflict to the Holocaust.

ZOE. I had family in the Holocaust too, Bekah.

REBEKAH. I actually didn't. My family is from Iran.

ZOE. Okay.

> *(A moment.)*

From Iran. You are from Iran then.

REBEKAH. Israel. I was born in Israel.

ZOE. And now you're here.

REBEKAH. Yeah.

ZOE. So you don't need to be there.

REBEKAH. I visit.

ZOE. But if you are living here, an Iranian Jew, others can too.

REBEKAH. You're dumb. Bye.

(REBEKAH starts to walk off – but then ZOE grabs her arm, pulling REBEKAH back.)

REBEKAH. Get off me.

(ZOE is holding REBEKAH's arm tight. Everyone else is looking on, completely rapt.)

ZOE. You are the problem.

REBEKAH. What are you – Oh my God.

(REBEKAH starts to walk off – but then ZOE grabs her arm, pulling REBEKAH back.)

Get off me.

(ZOE is holding REBEKAH's arm tight. Everyone else is looking on, completely rapt.)

ZOE. Jews are white! We are privileged!

(ZOE is playing tug of war with REBEKAH's arm. It's a very awkward fight.)

(ZOE won't let go.)

REBEKAH. Not every Jew is like you!

Not every Jew is safe, wherever they are. Like in Eygpt or Ethiopia or France. Jews are murdered going to a kosher market in Paris. They risk their lives for chicken.

Also we did win Israel fair and square.

WE DID.

(IZZY, SUZIE, JULIA, and ZOE are shocked.)

ZOE. You are a terrible human being! You're not human even!

(REBEKAH kicks ZOE off her, releasing herself from ZOE's grasp.)

(Just then, the **PRINCIPAL***, of uncertain age, walk on, witnessing the fight.)*

PRINCIPAL. STOP IT! Right now!

Are you okay, Zoe?

ZOE. No. Not really.

PRINCIPAL. Rebekah. My office. Now... And Zoe. To get the full story here.

Scene Five

(Blank void of digital communication. Rapid fire texting from **JULIA, SUZIE, GRACE, IZZY** *and* **ZOE.***)*

JULIA. OMG when she hit you

SUZIE. KICKED

JULIA. Lol right

ZOE. The Principal got it. Like knew that she was in the wrong.

GRACE. Ninja emoji

JULIA. Lol stop

IZZY. Could not have gone better. We were heard and then she showed herself

GRACE. Ninja emoji

JULIA. Stop sign

ZOE. I can actually bake if anyone needs help making something

SUZIE. I was thinking of just getting something at that new bakery. Is that bad

ZOE. No that's great!

(A moment.)

Honestly if you do the math, buying the sugar, butter, all the stuff to make cookies, costs more than just buying them already made

(A moment.)

ZOE. I'm such a Jew I know

SUZIE. What?

JULIA. Confused

ZOE. Like being cheap. Bad joke sorry

IZZY. Julia have you talked to Luke

GRACE. Cross emoji

JULIA. Grace actually stop or I'm removing you from the group chat

(*A moment.*)

IZZY. His parents are Nazis

JULIA. I'm over him!!

SUZIE. Do you think we should get security for the bake sale. Like will Israeli soliders show up lol jk

JULIA. Or her sister ugh. Grace why were you talking to her

GRACE. I literally ran into her cause I was looking at my phone

ZOE. I can't believe Bekah said we "won" Israel

JULIA. Zionism is evil

ZOE. This is why when people say being anti-zionist is being anti-Semitic I'm like why and also why I'm like why is it okay for me to not believe in God as a Jew but I have to believe in Israel why like why can you tell me no why

SUZIE. Does everyone know what they're baking bc some of you haven't signed up yet

GRACE. I'm getting muffins from Whole Foods

IZZY. Lol is anyone actually baking

SUZIE. We're raising money for Refugees United so it'd be good if someone did

JULIA. Why does it matter where the food comes from if we sell it

IZZY. I'm making pao de quejo

GRACE. Whats that

IZZY. Google Grace

> *(A moment. Then, **ARIEL** enters the blank void of digital communication.)*
>
> *(Everyone else's heads turn down and look at the phones, their faces lit up by the lights.)*
>
> *(**ARIEL** texts **GRACE**.)*

ARIEL. So funny literally running into you

> *(**GRACE** walks off.)*

Grace?

> *(**ARIEL** texts **JULIA**.)*

Hey Julia! Did you read *"Death of a Salesman"* yet for drama class

It's good

> *(**JULIA** walks off.)*

Suzie, I really want to support and help volunteer for the bake sale. I can like set up the tables if you want

> *(**SUZIE** walks off.)*

Izzy! You're totally right.

My sister is the most terrible human being ever

She's actually not human

She's a lizard

You can screenshot this text

(**IZZY** *walks off.*)

ARIEL. Zoe. Hi.

I'm really embarrassed.

Like, honestly I do believe in Israel. I know you don't and that's okay but my sister is not okay

Don't share this sorry I shouldn't said anything

(**ZOE** *walks off.*)

(**ARIEL** *is alone now. And she knows it. She's really frustrated.*)

(**ARIEL** *finally puts her phone away. She kicks around, just so angry, and UGH.*)

(**BEKAH** *is there, calmly reading a book. She's been there the whole time.*)

(**ARIEL** *turns to* **BEKAH**, *channelling her rage.*)

EVERYONE HATES ME NOW.

(**BEKAH** *doesn't respond.*)

BECAUSE OF YOU.

REBEKAH. I don't want anyone to know we're related either.

ARIEL. We don't even look alike! It's so unfair.

(**BEKAH** *doesn't respond.*)

Do you care? Do not care? Do you ANYTHING.

REBEKAH. Yeah I care that our school is full of anti-Semites.

(**REBEKAH** *is matter of fact about it.*)

They all hate you because they hate me.

ARIEL. You said something really terrible!

REBEKAH. We did win Israel. There was a war. This has gone on for all history. We lost it, like centuries ago, and then – we won our land back. Everyone is jealous because that doesn't really happen anymore. Like Indigenous people don't get their land back.

ARIEL. We're not Indigenous.

REBEKAH. We are to Israel.

ARIEL. Like 5,000 years ago.

REBEKAH. Yeah. Exactly.

ARIEL. They don't hate Zoe. So it's not anti-Semitism. It's because I am related to a racist.

REBEKAH. Um I'm not racist but even if I was why should they hate you because of it?

>*(A moment. **ARIEL** tries to think of what to say.)*

ARIEL. I wish the school didn't suspend you. I wish they expelled you and forced you to go boarding school. In Switzerland. So you would learn to mind your own business!

REBEKAH. K.

ARIEL. UGGgggghGGGAHHHH!!!

>*(**ARIEL** takes a pillow and hits **BEKAH**.)*

REBEKAH. See. We're a very violent people. You're proving their point.

ARIEL. You're wrong. You're the wrong one.

>*(**ARIEL** is enraged. But she's trying to hold it in.)*

ARIEL. And Imma and Abba are going to talk with the Principal and make it worse.

REBEKAH. Yea I know. They think the whole thing is screwed up. Like about the bake sale. Nothing's wrong with standing up for your people. Even though you obviously can't.

ARIEL. Everyone is going to hate us more now.

REBEKAH. If they're going to attack me, I'm going to attack them.

ARIEL. You started it.

REBEKAH. No I didn't.

ARIEL. Yes you did.

REBEKAH. No I didn't.

ARIEL. Yes you did.

*(***BEKAH*** hits ***ARIEL*** with a pillow. Hard.)*

OW. WHAT THE.

(A moment.)

Whatever. A pillow doesn't really hurt. Idiot.

REBEKAH. Shut up or I'm going smother you to death.

(A stand off.)

*(***BEKAH*** grips the pillow. ***ARIEL*** flinches.)*

Scene Six

(As the scene transitions, an announcement comes from the loud speaker. It's LUKE.)

LUKE'S VOICE. *(Offstage.)* Don't forget to sign up for the bake sale. I'm making some hot tamales, come at me.

(The classroom. Same one as Scene One.)

(JULIA, SUZIE and IZZY are there. Organizing the bake sale.)

JULIA. Can either of you actually bake?

SUZIE. Yeah?

JULIA. Because I know that I signed up to bring croissants but they're actually really hard to get right and I don't think I should do it if I can't get it right.

(IZZY is looking at the sign-up sheet.)

IZZY. Monica Fisher is making churros. Is that right?

SUZIE. Her mom is from Mexico.

(ZOE busts into the room.)

ZOE. Why aren't you answering your texts? Did you see what I wrote?

(They look at ZOE, confused. Then at their phones.)

(IZZY shoots up from her chair.)

IZZY. Her parents!? They cancelled the bake sale! What the. WHAT.

SUZIE. I've worked so hard – we've all been working so hard.

SUZIE. So that's it. It's over. All this hard work – and the money we were going to raise for refugees.

IZZY. I thought Jews cared about refugees.

(To **ZOE.***)*

Isn't that your culture?

SUZIE. Like when that terrible scum person went and shot all those Jews in Pittsburgh. Because they were supporting refugees.

ZOE. Yeah.

(A moment.)

JULIA. I don't get it. How do they – like her parents have the power?

SUZIE. ...Her mom is very...Loud.

ZOE. That's how Israelis are. It's embarrasing.

IZZY. Her parents also have a lot of money.

ZOE. I know. They're like every bad Jewish stereotype come to life. I am actually ashamed.

SUZIE. Oh no. Should we not being saying this? I honestly don't know Jewish triggers.

(A moment. **ZOE** *thinks.)*

ZOE. Well, um. I wouldn't say like, to the Principal, or anyone else, about the money thing.

IZZY. Her parents do have a lot of money. That's true.

Her mom has this big job at that tech company.

ZOE. Right, no, I'm just saying that – "All Jews are rich" is like a thing anti-Semites do say. So just be careful. Like, yea some Jews have a lot of money. I don't.

IZZY. Your dad works at a bank.

ZOE. Right but we're still not rich. There are a lot of jobs at banks.

IZZY. That pay really well. It's fine. My mom is a lawyer who makes a lot of money. And donates a lot of it. We shop at Target for everything.

ZOE. That's why I love you, Izzy.

You're better than me.

IZZY. No you're great too, Zoe.

(*ZOE pauses for a moment.*)

JULIA. Sometimes I feel like we're just talking and not doing anything.

(*JULIA feels a buzz on her phone. They all do. They look at their phones.*)

Grace.

SUZIE. She said Bekah is here. At school.

ZOE. With her parents?

IZZY. We all got the same text, Zoe. We don't know anything more.

(*They all get another text.*)

JULIA. Her sister is crying.

IZZY. See I told you she was trouble too.

(*Suddenly, ARIEL is there. Right at the door. She wants to come in. They all look at ARIEL.*)

ARIEL. Why do you hate me?

IZZY. We don't anything you. We don't know you.

ARIEL. (*To JULIA.*) Julia. We were in *RENT* together.

ZOE. We're not friends, Ariel. Like was I at your Bat Mitzvah? No because we're not friends.

ARIEL. No one actually knows where hummus is really from. Like I mean not here but like maybe Greece, or Egypt. Not Palestine.

IZZY. Ariel. Please leave.

ARIEL. I am just saying that it's a food and its roots are like – I mean yes Middle Eastern, or maybe Greek, but it is a food that is now Israeli too just like, hamburgers are from Germany actually but like, they're now American. Hamburg Germany. Hamburger.

IZZY. This is about your sister saying that all Arabs are terrorists. Do you not get that?

ARIEL. I don't agree with her.

ZOE. But it is true that hummus isn't Israeli. Because Israel has only existed since 1948 and hummus been around in Arab countries forever. So.

ARIEL. You only like Zoe because she just agrees with you to the point that she...like Zoe you're an anti-Semite. You are.

ZOE. Because I don't think Jews should be in Palestine?

SUZIE. Defending Israel is defending genocide.

ARIEL. No.

IZZY. "No." Okay.

SUZIE. You are defending genocide.

ARIEL. It's not.

IZZY. You are killing Palestinians. You are! That is fact.

ARIEL. They're trying to kill us.

IZZY. WOW.

ARIEL. But I'm not killing anyone. I mean if you'd ask me, I want peace.

(**ARIEL** *looks like she could cry.*)

IZZY. Now you're crying!?

> (**ARIEL** *tries hold her tears in.*)

ZOE. Ariel oh my God, you're just – you're younger than us so that's why.

ARIEL. That's why you hate me?

ZOE. We don't anything you. We don't think about you. We don't care. We're just angry. At this whole thing.

Scene Seven

(The hallway.)

(BEKAH *is back at school now. She walks down the lonely corridor – until she runs into* **LUKE.***)*

LUKE. ¡Hola mi amiga!

REBEKAH. Hi.

LUKE. I thought you were kicked out.

REBEKAH. No.

LUKE. Everyone's been chisme-ing about you. And the chisme is that la principal said adios.

REBEKAH. Since when do you speak Spanish?

Because you sound stupid.

LUKE. Bekah have you ever thought that people don't like you because you're mean?

REBEKAH. Yeah.

LUKE. You know this whole thing is stupido. That's stupid en Español.

REBEKAH. Please stop. With the Spanish.

LUKE. So they don't like you because you're mean right? But they also hate you because you're Jewish.

REBEKAH. They love Zoe.

LUKE. Yeah and Zoe really hates Jews.

I'm the only one on your side you know that right?

REBEKAH. You don't answer my texts.

LUKE. My parents and all their friends from church called the Principal. And they said that the Jews have a birthright to Israel.

REBEKAH. I asked if we could hang out soon.

LUKE. Yeah of course we can.

My parents actually – they were wondering if you could speak to our church.

REBEKAH. I didn't ask for your parents to call.

LUKE. We know you didn't! But you know, we saw a wrong and wanted to make it right. Israel is the Jewish homeland. It is. And there's nothing wrong with you telling people that.

REBEKAH. But like, why did you do this whole big thing for me and then not make plans with me.

LUKE. I didn't do this for you. My parents, it was their idea.

REBEKAH. To cancel?

LUKE. No to stand up for Israel! For Jews! And you know B, I did think you'd be happy about it.

(**BEKAH** *is not happy.*)

We can hang out on Sunday after church if you want. Or you can come to church too.

REBEKAH. Now everyone is going to think my parents cancelled the bake sale, when it was yours.

LUKE. Oye what you need is some pride. Your blood is in that soil. Your ashes make up that sand.

REBEKAH. That's what white supremacists say, Luke.

LUKE. Maybe los judeos son los blancos supremos. That's why everyone is scared of you.

(**BEKAH** *doesn't know how to respond.*)

LUKE. Own it!

I don't know why you don't all own it.

Jews are only 2 percent of the U.S. population, yet 7 percent of Congress is Jewish.

More than a quarter of the 400 billionaires on the Forbes list are Jews.

You do run Hollywood. You literally started it. And Stephen Spielberg taught America about the Holocaust.

And so many people in Hollywood are Jewish and you probably don't even realize it.

Like, Timothée Chalamet. And he's really hot, according to like girls and gay guys and screw it, me too.

Jews own banks. Yo do you know Goldman Sachs? Or what about the OG Rothschild.

They literally invented banks.

And coffee. Starbucks, Dunkin Donuts.

Ice cream. Actually I am going to boycott Ben and Jerry's but just cause they're traitors.

How about instead of saying you don't run the world be like Beyonce and say who runs the world?

Jews.

Who runs the world?

Jews.

Who runs the world?

Jews.

C'mon. Get into it.

> (*In the middle of* **LUKE** *going on and on,* **ARIEL** *trenches on stage, wiping away the last*

of her tears, followed by **ZOE**, *who is trying to get her attention.)*

*(***ARIEL*** and* **ZOE** *hears a bit of what Luke says, are both like what the...)*

ZOE. See this is exactly why I'd just – rather be...a basic white girl.

REBEKAH. ... Yeah sometimes...same.

ARIEL. Same.

*(***LUKE*** looks at* **BEKAH** *and* **ARIEL**, *examining them.)*

LUKE. But aren't you two from Iran?

End of Play

HATCH

by C. Quintana

HATCH premiered on May 20th, 2022 and was produced by the Keen Company. The performance was directed by Lynne Marie Rosenberg. The cast was as follows:

AIO . . . . Quinn Canales
BERNIE . . . . Shoshana Hoover
ROBIN . . . . Tovi Lisker
KAI . . . . Diego Martinez
SLOANE . . . . Zane Elinson
FRESHMAN . . . . Brendan O'Connell
HATCHIE . . . . Brendan O'Connell
HATCHOO . . . . Elyana Rodriguez
HATCHER . . . . Nicole Noriega
HATCHATA . . . . Ellis Jablonski
HATCHUM . . . . Anthony Tesis

CHARACTERS

The Students/Drama Crew

AIO – an aspiring actor and current senior who plays the lead

BERNIE – a budding production stage manager who takes their job very seriously

ROBIN – a class clown type, totally crushing on Sloane

KAI – the sincere playwright for the current production – their first play!

SLOANE – a team player who is kind of just along for the ride

FRESHMAN – a nosy underclassman, to be doubled by one of the Hatches (probably Hatchie)

The Hatches *(A kooky Greek chorus of sorts)*

HATCHIE – exuberant attention-seeker, Sloane's opposite

HATCHOO – silly, Bernie's opposite

HATCHER – matter of fact, Robin's opposite

HATCHATA – sardonic, Kai's opposite

HATCHUM – congenial people pleaser, Aio's opposite

SETTING

Your Recently Reopened High School Theatre/Auditorium.

Today. Now.

AUTHOR'S NOTES

There is magic here. Status quo. Enough said.

Note: This play can be about a high school theater space re-opening post COVID-19 pandemic closures, or perhaps after a natural disaster, or for another viable reason. In any case, what's important is that the students have been kept from the space for a substantial amount of time and are anxious/psyched to be back in the theater!

Production Notes

All names chosen are androgynous for a reason and therefore can be played by actors of any gender, ability, ethnicity, or race, however, it is ESSENTIAL – please and thank you, to fill this play up with a variety of all of the above! Plentiful POC performers! Plentiful queer performers! Plentiful performers of varying abilities! Hooray!

The (/) slashes indicate when a line is cut off and the next character begins speaking. Be liberal.

In the wonderful words of Lynne Rosenberg: "The hatches confuse and create madness, but they don't lie!"

(The jangle of keys and the entrance to the theater opens, perhaps there is a ghost light on stage. Otherwise, the space is empty.)

BERNIE. OK! That's the peek! You saw it. Terrific. We'll be back tomorrow for spacing and dress rehearsal.

(Everyone walks past **BERNIE** *and into the space.)*

Hey! Hello! Did you hear what I just said? / It's a *peek* not an *inspection.*

KAI. Come on, Bern. You can't just open the door and expect us not to look around –

SLOANE. It's been – *forever* –

AIO. I can't believe we're back.

(Shouts into the empty theater.)

We're back!

ALL HATCHES. *(Offstage.) (An echo the students don't hear, but we do.)* Back Back Back!

KAI. I really missed this place – didn't you, Bernie?

BERNIE. Well, yeah, of course I did – but it wasn't safe! They had to clear the mold from the vents/ before we could–

AIO.	**SLOANE.**
Gross…	Are we *sure* it's clear? It still kind of smells funny…

ROBIN. Our whole school smells funny…kind of like vintage farts.

SLOANE. Ever think maybe it's *you* and not the school?

ROBIN. *(To* **SLOANE** *– clear flirtation happening here.)* Could just as easily be you.

BERNIE. Or the mold.

> *(***AIO** *steps downstage, taking in the darkened audience.)*

AIO. It's going to be *incredible* to perform again for a live audience in here –

KAI. Let's hope they like the play...

BERNIE. OK – this was great, and everything, but we should probably get out of here. It's *very dark* –

SLOANE.	**ROBIN.**
Just use the flashlight on your phone –	Ooooh! Could be haunted!

AIO.	**SLOANE.**
(Puts cell phone flashlight on.) Smart.	Who would want to haunt this place?

ROBIN. Aren't theaters, like, the number one places for ghosts to haunt?

KAI.	**SLOANE.**	**AIO.**
Definitely.	Maybe...	Where are the house lights...?

> *(***AIO** *wanders backstage in search of the lights.)*

BERNIE. OK, EVERYONE! Listen up! As the *production stage manager*, I have been entrusted with the keys, and I don't take that responsibility lightly!

KAI. *(Re:* **BERNIE.***)* Groan.

AIO. *(Calls from backstage.)* I can't figure out the lights. / Were they always this complicated?

ROBIN. Why don't you ask the *production stage manager*?

KAI. *(To* **BERNIE.***)* Well, Bernie...?

ALL HATCHES. *(Offstage.) (Again, unheard by the students.)* Bernie?

> *(After a beat of anticipation –.)*

BERNIE. I don't know, Kai. I – I've never actually stage managed before – not like this.

> *(Gets quiet.)*

It's different with Zoom theatre...

> *(Obnoxious house lights turn on overhead. Like, ouch, my-eyes-hurt-bright.)*

AIO. *(Shouts.)* Got 'em!

> *(***BERNIE*** almost trips over the lock on the stage's trap door.)*

BERNIE. You're supposed to call "LIGHTS" <u>before</u> you turn the lights on or off to warn the cast and crew – that's standard theatrical protocol!!!

AIO. *(Entering.)* Lights.

BERNIE. *(Recovering from the fall or near fall.)* Thanks...

KAI. Whoa! I totally forgot this theater has a trap door!

ROBIN. You mean a *trip* door...

SLOANE. *(Re:* **ROBIN***'s bad joke.)* No.

AIO. How come we never use it?

BERNIE. For what? Our school's not exactly producing *Phantom of the Opera* anytime soon.

SLOANE. So...what's the point, then?

AIO. A trap door is *perfect* for a *really* dramatic entrance! Kai – maybe we can incorporate it into the show somehow? I think it would really make sense for my character –

KAI. Yeah, uh, maybe, but it doesn't really work/ in the context of the play –

BERNIE. Well, it's locked, anyway,/ so there's nothing we can do!

AIO. Are you/ sure?

BERNIE. What a shame. I guess we'll just have to go on our way. Nothing to see here, folks... Aren't you getting hungry? I'm really getting hungry. I didn't eat lunch!

SLOANE.	ROBIN.
Nah. I'm not really hungry.	*(To* **BERNIE,** *genuinely concerned.)* Hey. Why didn't you eat lunch?

AIO. *(Re: the lock.)* Yeah – I'd rather open this thing. / I still think we should use it –

BERNIE. You realize all that you're going to find down there is a bunch of dust and old props, so really there's no reason to even try/ – it's just a waste of time.

KAI. Have you even been down there before?

BERNIE. Well, no... /but there's *clearly* a reason it's locked.

KAI. You must be a *little* curious.

BERNIE. Not at all. There could be hazardous materials down there.

ROBIN. What is it – dust or hazardous waste? **(ANNOUNCER** *voice.) The world may never know...*

SLOANE. Why would there be hazardous waste below a theater trap door?

BERNIE. Why would there be mold in a ventilation system?

SLOANE. Moisture?

BERNIE. *(Annoyed.)* We can't take any chances! As the production stage manager it's my responsibility to be aware of potential safety issues –

AIO. I guess we *could* just ask Ms. Doody to show us in rehearsal tomorrow.

BERNIE. That, Aio, is an excellent/ idea –

SLOANE. Ugh. I can't believe her parents *actually* named her Judy – Judy Doody. It's cruel.

ROBIN. And also kind of hilarious.

KAI. You're not wrong.

AIO. *(Re: the trap door.)* So, we open it, right?

KAI.	ROBIN.	SLOANE.	BERNIE.
Yeah.	Definitely.	Let's do it.	*No!*

> *(Suddenly the trap door starts to rumble and shake – like there's a monster locked beneath. Terrifying. The group all circles around the trap door. Maybe someone grabs the ghost light as a weapon –.)*

ROBIN.	BERNIE.	KAI.	SLOANE.
What the –	How –?	Is there something down there?!	UM –

> *(Then, just as quickly as the shaking began, a bubblegum nostalgic sort of pop song erupts from the trap door.* **ROBIN** *inadvertently rocks out – and they may not be the only one. Come on, it's catchy!)*

---

* A license to produce *Hatch* does not include a performance license for any third-party or copyrighted music. Licensees should create an original composition or use music in the public domain. For further information, please see the Music and Third-Party Materials Use Note on page iii.

BERNIE. Robin? Are you doing this!? It's not funny!

ROBIN. I – I – *no*. I mean I – I love this song, but *no*.

SLOANE. You did run sound that one time –

ROBIN. With my phone!

> *(Shows them – it's just his home screen, nothing else.)*

Look. Nothing!

KAI. Weird…

BERNIE. Well, Aio! Look what you've done!

AIO. I didn't do anything!

> *(Suddenly, the music goes silent.)*

SLOANE. *(To the trap door.)* Hello?! Is anyone down there? If so, give us a signal.

> **(ROBIN** *sings one or two lines from a song that begins with "Hello" or any other type of greeting.*)*

> **(SLOANE** *hushes* **ROBIN.** *They all lean in for an answer. A beat. None comes.)*

SLOANE. Oh my god. This is just like that show on Netflix about those high school kids stuck in that creepy guy's basement –

KAI. *Is it?*

ROBIN. Which one?

SLOANE. *(Ominous.)* None of them turn out well…

AIO. *(To the hatch door.)* Hello, whoever's down there! We're here to help!

SLOANE. Are we?

BERNIE. We're kind of jumping to conclusions here, aren't we? Do they really *need* help? It sort of sounded like... like...

AIO. A party?

KAI. Parties *can* be dangerous.

SLOANE. *(Genuine.)* Yeah, like that *Crucible* opening night party –

KAI. "I saw Goody Proctor with the devil."

SLOANE. *(Shivers.)* Can't unsee it.

AIO. *(To everyone.)* Hey. What do you think the code is for the lock?

BERNIE. Why? There's *no* reason/ to try to open it –

ROBIN. Maybe, like 1-2-3-4?

SLOANE. Robin. That's the stupidest combination I've ever heard.

(AIO tries it.)

AIO. It worked!

(ROBIN shrugs.)

SLOANE. You're kidding...

ROBIN. What can I say I–

SLOANE. Got really lucky.

AIO. Can y'all help me out? This thing is *heav-y.*

BERNIE. Why are we doing this again?!

SLOANE. Yeah, come to think of it, I'm not really in the mood to meet an axe murderer. Why are we doing this again?

AIO. Because actors should make active choices, right?

KAI.	BERNIE.
Really?	I'm not an actor.

AIO. *(To* BERNIE.*)* But you *do* want us to lift this thing as safely as possible, don't you?

ROBIN. *What Would Judy Do...oody?*

> *(A beat, they ignore* ROBIN, *then all look to* BERNIE, *and then:)*

BERNIE. Fine, fine. We open it, *then we go.*

AIO.	SLOANE.	ROBIN.	KAI.
Yeah! Of course.	OK ...	Sounds good to me.	Open, then go.

> *(Together they heave the trap door open.* BERNIE *grumbles.)*
>
> *(A bright light emerges, entrancing them all.)*
>
> *(From within, they hear –.)*

HATCHUM. *(Calls from within.)* Hatchoo! Hatchoo! Hatchooooooooo!

ROBIN. *(Calls back.)* Bless you!

KAI. I actually don't think that was a sneeze...

AIO. I'm going in.

BERNIE. You're what!? We said open, then *go! We all agreed!*

SLOANE. Maybe Bernie's right –

BERNIE. Thank you!

SLOANE. Maybe we should –

> *(It's too late.)*

(Wild, canned backwards applause followed by a loud magical sound follows –.)

*(Suddenly, **AIO** is gone and has somehow pulled everyone along with them.)*

(We are in another world – under the theater, inside of the trap space.)

*(The **HATCHES** perform an eerie synchronized dance of sorts to welcome the drama crew down below.)*

AIO. This would slay on TikTok. / Damn, why won't my phone –

*(Before **AIO** has enough time to fully grasp their phone not working, **HATCHOO** distracts them.)*

HATCHOO. Hellooooo!

HATCHUM. FINALLY! You made it. We've been trying to get your attention for millions upon millions of seconds. Too many seconds to count, really.

HATCHIE. *(To **SLOANE**.)* How many seconds in a year?

SLOANE. *(Looks to the others.)* Uh. I have no idea…

HATCHIE. 12! Get it!?

SLOANE. No?

HATCHOO. January 2nd, February 2nd, March 2nd – and on it goes!

BERNIE. Um – hi?

HATCHIE. I'm Hatchie! The baby!

HATCHER. Hatcher! Hiya.

HATCHATA. *Hatchata.*

HATCHUM. Hatchum.

HATCHOO. Hatchoo!

> (**BERNIE** *sneezes from the dust – it sounds like*
> *"achoo!".)*

HATCHOO. Yes! *Hatchoo!*

BERNIE. No, I was just – I have allergies, it's very dusty/ –
never mind...

AIO. *(To the* **HATCHES.***) What is this place?*

HATCHER. Why, you're just down the hatch, of course.

HATCHIE. *In the trap?!*

> *(A riff or two of trap music magically plays.)*

ROBIN. *(Re: the music, maybe points up to the sound.)* Ha.
Nice!

AIO. And this is...what exactly?

ROBIN. It's *trap* music.

BERNIE. Not the music!

HATCHUM. It's pretty simple! We're your foils.

KAI. Like, our *narrative* foils? Our opposites?

HATCHOO.	**HATCHER.**	**HATCHUM.**
(To **BERNIE.***)*	*(To* **ROBIN.***)*	*(Re:* **KAI.***)* Ah.
Yep yep yep.	That's right.	You're the
		playwright!

ALL THE HATCHES. Mmm.

BERNIE. This isn't happening because of the mold – is it?

HATCHOO. Nope!

ROBIN. So...what exactly is happening right now?

HATCHER. It's like this in every theater! There are Hatches for every play, every cast and crew member of every production ever.

AIO. Really?

HATCHOO. *(To* **BERNIE.***)* Ever ever, Trevor.

BERNIE. My name's not Trevor.

HATCHOO. Clever!

HATCHIE. It gets better!

SLOANE. Wait. So, you're telling us there's some other dimension underneath every single theater in America?

HATCHIE. *(Echo effect.)* THE WHOLE WORLD-WORLD-WORLD-WORLD!

KAI. *What?* How?! I don't think I understand what's going on –

ALL THE HATCHES. No one understands what's going on.

SLOANE. I *definitely* don't understand what's going on.

ALL THE HATCHES. You definitely *don't* understand what's going on!

> *(The* **HATCHES** *all laugh – each of them in their own way.* **HATCHOO***'s is more of a yelp,* **HATCHUM***'s more of a chortle.)*

BERNIE. Right... So. You all seem fine, so I guess we can go back up to the theater?

HATCHUM. Technically *this* is the theater, too.

BERNIE. Right, but – I mean, up there. I have to return the keys to Ms. Doody.

HATCHIE. Ha-ha-ha-ha-ha-ha-ha-ha!

HATCHOO. Good luck with that!

(**BERNIE** *tries to find an escape – there is none as far as they can tell. They're in a strange void…*)

BERNIE. *We're not even supposed to be in here*, but now I have no idea how we get out!

HATCHUM. You're right! It's quite the conundrum.

HATCHER. Why leave? It's nice here.

HATCHATA.	**HATCHIE.**
(Sarcastic.) Oh yeah. Luxurious.	*(Genuine.)* Cozy!

HATCHOO. I am the beginning of the end, the end of every place. I am the beginning of eternity, the end of time and space! What am I?

KAI. It's a riddle.

HATCHATA. *(Claps, deadpan.)* Congratulations. You're a genius.

HATCHOO. I am the beginning of the end, the end of every place. I am the beginning of eternity, the end of time and space! What am I?

ROBIN. I don't know? Frustrating?

KAI. Wait! I think it means – we're at the *end* of the play!

BERNIE.	**SLOANE.**
Why?	I guess that makes sense?

HATCHER.	**HATCHOO.**
Sure!	Sense!

HATCHUM. Why not?

HATCHER. *We've* been in limbo. In the dark theater. Waiting for the show to begin…

HATCHATA. And it *hasn't*.

HATCHUM. The beginning is where the show starts!

HATCHIE. It's the only way!

HATCHER. Otherwise, no dress rehearsal, no opening night –

BERNIE. Wait! *Our dress rehearsal?/ Our opening night?*

AIO. <u>No way.</u> There *has* to be. We've been waiting for this *a long time*. I'm a senior – I won't get any more chances.

HATCHATA. Then I guess you'd better find a solution.

HATCHUM. You help us, we help you, eh?

HATCHOO. Batter up. Take us home!

KAI. Wait. So – we're at the end of the play as in *my* play?

HATCHATA. What other play?

KAI. I, mean, there are lots of plays...

HATCHIE. Not now! There's only one play here, in this moment! Underneath this theater!

HATCHER. Remember the final scene?

HATCHOO. The death scene!

AIO. Of course! I'm an actor – I'm the lead.

ALL THE HATCHES. You're an actor! The lead!

KAI. Wait. There's a death scene?

AIO. ...Um. Weird...For some reason I can't remember any of my lines.

SLOANE. Huh. I can't remember mine either!

ROBIN. Me neither...

BERNIE. But we're off book! The off-book deadline was ages ago! We have a dress rehearsal *tomorrow*!

HATCHOO. Well, maybe you do, maybe you don't?

BERNIE.   **AIO.**

We do.   We do.

ROBIN. You wrote it, Kai. What's the end of the play?

KAI. *(Struggling to remember. What is going on?!)* Um...
yeah...I, of course...I...

Well, if it's a death scene. Then maybe we just need to
die?

SLOANE. Which one of us?

ROBIN. All of us?

BERNIE. Yes!

> *(They all fall to the ground and "die." The*
> **HATCHES** *look on, walk around them. They're*
> *delighted by the madness.)*

> *(A beat or two of the group "being dead,"*
> *then –.)*

SLOANE. *(Rises.)* I don't think that worked.

ROBIN. Now what?

HATCHIE. Try something else!

HATCHATA. *(Dry.)* Please, let it be as riveting as the last.

AIO. Maybe it's just me? Like, maybe I need to die alone?
Since I'm the lead. Right?

KAI. Right.

ROBIN. Maybe we should explore a little bit. These guys
are wild, this place is dope – I'm in no rush to get
home...

SLOANE.   **BERNIE.**

(To **ROBIN**.*)* Are things   *(To everyone.)* I am. We
still.../with your folks?   need to return the keys
                                before Ms. Doody leaves.

ROBIN. Yeah. It's not great...

BERNIE. *(To* **ROBIN,** *insistent.) You can come to my house.*

SLOANE. Or mine...

ROBIN. *(Lights up, to* **SLOANE.)** Yeah?

HATCHER. The only way out of the trap is through the world of the play!

BERNIE. The world of the play?

KAI. It's *my* play... I think.

HATCHER. It's all our play.

HATCHIE. Everything is the play. The play is everything!

KAI. Then why can't we remember anything about it?

HATCHUM. That's just the way things go here.

SLOANE. That doesn't make sense.

HATCHOO. Nothing makes sense! Harumph!

SLOANE. But – wait a minute – let me get this straight. You've been waiting underneath the trap door all this time for us? Like, what if we had never come?

HATCHIE. That would have plain sucked.

HATCHER. It's true.

HATCHUM. We've waited a long time.

HATCHER. If the play doesn't go on, *we* don't go on.

HATCHOO.	**HATCHIE.**
Go on.	Gulp.

HATCHER. We *love* what we do, and if we can't do it –

HATCHATA. We're screwed.

BERNIE. How exactly does time operate down here? Just out of curiosity – because, if we're talking, we return and magically-no-time-has-passed, then great. I'm all good. But if not, *then* things are going to get a little dicey. I mean, I ride the bus home, so...if I miss the bus...

AIO. I'll give you a ride.

BERNIE. Right, but – like, do we think that'll be today? Tomorrow?

HATCHOO. Today! Tomorrow!

BERNIE. First of all, I've got low blood sugar and I'm not seeing any healthy snacks in sight. Second, we've got dress rehearsal tomorrow. *Invited dress.* With an audience! For Kai's *debut* play. For your *triumphant* return to the stage, Aio! The final performance of your *senior* year! And a little bird told me that a prominent Artistic Associate of a notable regional theater might be in the audience tomorrow night!

KAI. Really?

BERNIE. That's what Ms. Doody said.

ROBIN. Did she? *(Aside.)* And do you really have low blood sugar? Cuz the no eating thing – I've got a granola bar...

      *(**SLOANE** pulls out their cell phone.)*

SLOANE. *(Re: cell phone.)* Weird. I just realized I've got no service...

      (They all check their phones, and it's the same.)

HATCHUM. Yeah, that thing won't work here.

      *(**HATCHOO** swats it out of **SLOANE**'s hands.)*

SLOANE. Hey! What are you doing!?

HATCHOO. Blehhhhhh. Phoney baloney.

HATCHER. It has nothing to do with the play!

HATCHIE. *Your* play! *Our* play!

HATCHUM. This is not a kitchen sink drama.

HATCHOO. *Or* a wireless device drama!

BERNIE. OK! Well then, let's get on with it already, so we can get back.

HATCHIE. ALL RIGHT! Attention! Curtain.

HATCHER. Set the scene!

HATCHOO. *(Makes a bugle sound.)* Da-da-da! Playwright!

(*A beat.*)

HATCHUM. *(To **KAI**.)* We're waiting for you!

KAI. Oh, um! Yeah, of course...Um...I, uh...there's a storm!

> (*The* **HATCHES** *create the ambiance of the storm. It can be very foley – thundersheets, etc. Also, everything is elevated here, so the following scenes can be super melodramatic in a fun way!*)

We're on a rooftop. Aio's character is in a horrible fight with Sloane's character, and they are ready to end it all –

(*A beat.*)

SLOANE. Wait – me? Or Aio?

KAI. *(Clears throat.)* You! I don't care. Go ahead! *Someone.*

AIO. *(In character.)* I am "Someone"!

SLOANE. *(Changing voice; in character.)* So, this is it? The end?

AIO. *Yes!*

SLOANE. I guess when you've ruined everything, you aren't left with many choices.

AIO. How does it feel to know that you drove me to it? You're heartless, but the truth is, you're always going to be heartless – there's no chance a heart could grow in that barren ribcage.

SLOANE. It's hard to believe I loved you once, but I guess... I was different then.

AIO. *You never loved me.*

SLOANE. If I never loved you would I even be here at all?

HATCHUM. Hmmmm. Wait wait wait. I don't think this is it.

HATCHIE. Nope.

HATCHER. Yes – a touch less melodramatic.

KAI. I don't think it's melodramatic.

HATCHATA. Ha!

(*Catching their response.*)

I mean...oh...really?

AIO. It does feel different than I remember it.

SLOANE. Are we sure there was a death scene?

HATCHER. Yes. Maybe. Uncertain.

HATCHOO. InDUbitably!

ROBIN. But, like, is it a *death death* scene. Like tragedy? Or, is it more like horror/slasher sort of thing? Or, is it like ah-ha-ha-ha-ha asburd-made you look, kind of thing?

KAI. I mean, we can try that.

SLOANE. Why not try them all?

ROBIN. I think there's time? Is there time?

BERNIE. Let's keep it moving!

HATCHOO. Mooo-Mooo-Mooooooooving.

KAI. OK, cool – yeah, absurd. I can do that. Totally. Like, um, that Beckett guy, right?

HATCHATA. Something like that.

ROBIN. Who is that again?

SLOANE. *(Pronounces the "t.")* The *Waiting for Godot* guy.

HATCHIE. *(American pronunciation; pronounces Guhdoh.)* Godot!

HATCHATA. *(Britich pronunciation; pronounces GODoh.)* GOD-ot.

BERNIE. OK. I think we're getting off track here. At this rate, we're never getting back...

HATCHUM. We want you to get back, too!

SLOANE. *(Not quite believing it.)* You do?

KAI. We're not writing *Waiting for Godot. That* play has already been written – we're writing something in the *style* of *Waiting for Godot*, right?

HATCHER. Right!

HATCHOO. Right-o, not Godot!

AIO. So, make it weird?

KAI. It's not just weird. It's *absurd.*

AIO. *(Looking to KAI.)* So...?

> *(KAI thinks for a minute, then –.)*

KAI. Madness...

AIO. Sadness.

SLOANE. Gladness.

ROBIN. Radness –

BERNIE. Stop! Stop! You're just rhyming! This isn't anything like *Waiting for Godot*.

SLOANE. And where's the death scene? Don't we need a death scene?

HATCHER. Maybe it wasn't a death scene?

HATCHUM. You're right –

HATCHATA. Maybe it was more of a metaphorical death.

AIO. Well, what does a metaphorical death look like? How the hell am I supposed to *act* that?

HATCHOO. I dunno!

HATCHIE. Beats me.

HATCHATA. *(Emphasis on "tor".) You're* the act*or*.

BERNIE. Do you "hatches" – or whoever you are – really know anything at all?

HATCHER. We know action –

HATCHUM. And conflict –

HATCHIE. And beat shifts –

HATCHATA. And endings.

HATCHER. We know tension –

HATCHUM. And climax –

HATCHIE. And language –

HATCHOO. Inventing!

HATCHATA. But do you recall? The greatest denouement of all?

BERNIE. WHAT THE HELL IS GOING ON HERE?!

*(**BERNIE***'s yelling takes the* **HATCHES** *aback.)*

(Suddenly, a warped voice from above – vaguely akin to a more audible version of the adults in the Peanuts *cartoons –.)*

MS. DOODY VOICE. *(Offstage.) (The first part of the speech is warped, unintelligible.)* [We all know that it's been a very difficult time for our students, and it's a special thing that we can be back in the theater altogether again as a community. Keep in mind that this is our very first performance for a public audience in the recently remediated space – it's only a dress rehearsal, so things are still very much in flux!]

(The following is the only part of the monologue we actually hear/understand.)

... And so, without further ado, I welcome you to our *first* public performance of this brand-new play by our own Kai L. Greene. Thank you for being part of our process!

*(***BERNIE*** jumps up and down to try to get a view of what's going on. It's impossible.)*

BERNIE. Wait, what!? They're starting!? How can they be starting without us? The invited dress is tomorrow – it's not supposed to be happening until *tomorrow*. Is it tomorrow?

HATCHIE. *Is it* tomorrow?

AIO. WAIT. If we're down here, and *you're* down here – then who's up there in the play? Who's playing my part? Who's playing *your part?* All the parts.

SLOANE. If that's the pre-show announcement, then we're not at the end of the play, we're at the *beginning of the play*.

BERNIE. Who preset the props? Who cued the cues?

ROBIN. *(To the* **HATCHES.***)* You... You lied to us.

HATCHOO. *(Serious for once.)* Nooooo!

AIO. Why would you do that?

HATCHIE. No lies, just fun! We like to play! It's called _a play_!

HATCHER. With all the sads, did you forget?

HATCHUM. Don't forget the riddle!

HATCHIE. Ahem! I am the beginning of the end, the end of every place. I am the beginning of eternity, the end of time and space! What am I?

ROBIN. Oh my god... I just realized...

SLOANE.	**BERNIE.**
What?	WHAT?!

ROBIN. The answer to the riddle is the letter "e."

KAI. Oh. I get it – the beginning of the *word* "end," and the end of the *word* "place." Same with eternity, time, and space...

SLOANE.	**BERNIE.**	**HATCHOO.**
Ohhhhhh.	You have GOT to be kidding me –	Ding ding ding ding ding!

HATCHATA. *(Sarcastic, to the others.)* They're quick, these ones.

> *(The **HATCHES** may all laugh at this in their various ways.)*

SLOANE. Wait. So, the end-of-the play-thing wasn't really *the thing*?

> *(**HATCHIE** shrugs.)*

HATCHIE. Oh, the play's *the thing!*

BERNIE. *(To the **HATCHES**.)* Who are you, *really?*

HATCHER. Like we said –

HATCHOO. I'm you!

BERNIE. I thought you said you were Hatchoo!?

HATCHOO. Hatchoo is you!

HATCHIE. We're all of you.

HATCHUM. It's true.

BERNIE. OK! Enough of this already. Get us out of this weird hatch-trap door horror show.

SLOANE. *(Honest.)* Haven't we been through enough? It's been a really messed up year as it is...

AIO. We're getting out of here. Come on everybody!

BERNIE. But how?

KAI. Like this –

> *(Gesturing to everyone.)*

Follow my lead, OK?

> *(Clears throat.)*

And then, the theater kids stomp their feet –

> *(They do.)*

And clap their hands –

> *(They do.)*

And snap their fingers all at once –

> *(The group all snaps their fingers at once. Well, except* **SLOANE.***)*

SLOANE. Sorry, I can't really snap...

KAI. It's fine! Just pretend –

KAI. They snap their fingers all at once, except Sloane, who pretends because they can't snap –

And then – like magic – the Hatches as if struck by the snaps themselves, shake. *Then shake again.* Their arms wave, like those inflatable tube men outside of car dealerships, and stumble backward, backward, backward. Then they <u>*melt*</u> into the ground and, as if they're slurped up by some gigantic straw, they <u>*disappear*</u> into oblivion!

And then the students *cheer* –

> (**KAI** *waits for them to cheer. Maybe clears their throat until they do. (Feel free to improvise if more is needed.)*

KAI. The students <u>cheer</u> – LOUDLY, BOLDLY, *ENTHUSIASTICALLY* –

BERNIE.	**SLOANE.**	**AIO.**	**ROBIN.**
Hooray!	Yeah!	Wooooo!!!	Party!

KAI. And one, by one, the students lift themselves from the great depths of Hatchlandia and crawl millimeter by millimeter, centimeter by centimeter, inch by inch, foot by foot, back to the stage. The stage where they will perform for the first time in a long time in less than 24 hours' time –

They do this together, because – yeah, the show must go on, but really, after everything, *we need it to* – and we are all so *beyond* ready to make some theatrical magic happen on this stage, our stage – finally. <u>*For an audience, in real time*</u>...

(The disco light and magic pop music from earlier plays again – and it's somehow even more magnificent.)*

(And before we know it, we're back in the empty theater. The ghost light still on.)

(A long beat.)

AIO. Did that just –

ROBIN. Yeah.

SLOANE. Weird.

KAI. Guess you can return the keys now, Bern.

BERNIE. Yeah. Guess so...

SLOANE. I still don't think I know exactly what that – *you know what?* Forget about it!

AIO. You think they're still down there?

KAI. Nah. We *vanquished* those G.D. tricksters.

AIO. You know what, *even* so, let's get out of here. Big day tomorrow. Better not to take any chances...

BERNIE. *(Under breath.)* If you had listened to me in the first place –

(Suddenly the door to the theater opens and a freshman walks in.)

FRESHMAN. WHOAAAAA! How did y'all get in here?

BERNIE. Actually. We were just leaving. Right, everybody?

---

* A license to produce *HATCH* does not include a performance license for any third-party or copyrighted music. Licensees should create an original composition or use music in the public domain. For further information, please see the Music and Third-Party Materials Use Note on page iii.

SLOANE.	KAI.	AIO.
Yep.	Yeah.	Gotta get home...

> *(The* **FRESHMAN** *ignores them and walks onto the stage, sees the trap door wide open.)*

FRESHMAN. Cool, cool. I just want to look around a little bit.

BERNIE. Wow. Do I just make people *not* want to listen – is that what it is?

ROBIN. Nah – I think it's mostly that people don't listen.

> *(The* **FRESHMAN** *has made their way onto the stage.)*

FRESHMAN. There's a trap door in here! *Wicked.*

ROBIN. *(Under their breath.)* We were thinking more *Phantom of the Opera,* but that works, too...

FRESHMAN. I wonder what's –

BERNIE.	AIO.
WAIT.	STOP. Don't.

SLOANE. Don't touch it. It's dangerous.

> *(The* **FRESHMAN** *laughs.)*

FRESHMAN. You're kidding, right?

ROBIN. Nope!

> *(Together, two of the crew close the door to the trap.)*

> *(***ROBIN** *replaces the lock.)*

FRESHMAN. Why are you guys freaking out? It's just a door, it's not/ like there's anything living down –

ROBIN. Just. I wouldn't...

SLOANE. Trust us.

KAI. Yeah. Let's go.

> *(***SLOANE*** reaches for ***ROBIN****'s hand. It's welcome.)*

AIO. Bernie, you got the lights?

BERNIE. Lights out.

ALL. Thank you, lights!

> *(The lights go out, and they leave the theater – until tomorrow!)*

End of Play

www.ingramcontent.com/pod-product-compliance
Lightning Source LLC
Chambersburg PA
CBHW070334120726
47909CB00008B/2690